TRAPUNZEL

TANZANIA GLOVER

Cover Art by Bree Taylor Design

www.tanzaniaglover.com

I dedicate this to any woman who is still trying to find herself.

To the lovely Dionne Richard. Thanks for being a great friend and letting me play in your life for this story even though it's actually nothing like your life.

PREFACE

Okay so technically my experiment to write a series of novellas may have failed, but I think what I produced instead was even better. I'm so thankful for every single reader who has taken this journey with me because writing this series and connecting with you ladies over the last year was one of the most exciting and rewarding things I've ever done.

My intention for this particular fairytale was to show that it's never too late to find yourself or love if that's what you want. I also wanted to show that Happily Ever After looks differently for everyone and they don't all have to follow the same formula.

Enjoy and don't forget to check out the carefully curated playlist that complements this magical tale!

TRAPUNZEL

1

TRAP QUEEN

NICOLE

First off I'm a whole hypocrite and I'm not anybody's role model so don't ever try to do the shit that I do and expect the same results. And now that we got that out of the way we can get down to the nitty gritty.

If you asked my mama Winnie Mae she would tell you I was born with an attitude and a slick mouth. But after getting my ass beat one time too many on the playground because of it, I asked my daddy Henry Lou to teach me how to fight.

I was too small to do much damage to an opponent, but he did what he could and showed me how to catch a bigger person off guard by standing on their feet and going to town with my fists before they even realized the fight had started. It wasn't proper fight protocol at all, but he told me if I was fighting it was *to win* not *to be fair.* It worked too because I hadn't taken an ass whooping since.

These days I wasn't much of a fighter anymore, but I stayed at the gun range and I never missed if anybody had a problem with me that couldn't be solved in a minute or two. Thankfully I'd only had to use it once at a gas station years ago because some disrespectful nigga couldn't keep his hands to himself.

I just grazed him a little on purpose, but after word got out that little Nicole Jones was legally packing *and didn't bust back but shot first*, I never had to pull my little pocket Glock out again.

That's when the folks in Fulton County started saying that I hated men. And they weren't wrong because for as long as I could remember I truly had. And I knew a lot of women started saying that shit after a few niggas had played Hot Potato with their hearts, but it had been a long time since my heart was broken and I still couldn't stand their trifling asses.

Among other things I guess my main aversion to them came because like most girls I'd fallen for the first boy who made me laugh and then the second and the third until I decided that the heartbreaks weren't worth the laughs because that's what comedians were for.

And while I was at it, I might as well add in that at some point most women were gonna have to just admit that they liked being played because when it came to matters of the heart, nine times out of ten we knew the man wasn't shit immediately so we were no longer just innocent victims being led to slaughter. We were volunteers. My dumb ass got played a few times and decided that I didn't like it so now I didn't get played anymore. That's literally all that had to be done because these men would forever be about games and the only way for us to win at them was not to play at all.

Unfortunately I didn't know many women who thought like I did so I was mostly alone in that regard. Even my best friend Tillar, who knew better by proxy just off the strength of being my friend, was still a hopeless romantic and intent on finding "Mr. Right" for years.

She had been emotionally banged up from one relationship after another, but no matter how much she wanted to she couldn't just occasionally smash like I did because she still craved these niggas romantically.

"Yeah I know most of them are trash, but I just need one to act right, Nic. One."

I had never let that side of her interfere with our friendship though even when it had gotten exhausting letting her use my shoulder to cry on after every breakup, especially because I had seen that shit coming from a mile away. But I was always a little offbeat as the only child to older, devoutly religious parents and she was my first *real* friend so no matter what I wasn't ever letting her go.

And no doubt I annoyed her sometimes too because she didn't give a damn about comic books or any of the manga and anime shit I was into, but she would let me talk about it for hours whenever something major happened. She had even started coming around to the big movie premieres since I dragged her to all of them on account of me not liking to go alone.

I thought that doing stuff like that might come to an end when her now husband Cam moved in, but he was always happy to be our third wheel and equally happy to stay home when we needed our quality time. Plus his tall, Jolly Green Giant ass scared off most men so he was like built in, free security and that always came in handy.

Like for instance, literally just a minute ago on this fine February day some ignorant fool had decided to test my gangsta by coming into Thread and asking for *FreakNic*. That was the nickname I was given by a few clown ass Ques from Morehouse back in the day, but I could tell that the only classes this drunk, country negro had ever been enrolled in was for the remedial.

But before he could even take a step in my direction behind the register, Cam, who was only in the boutique to put up some new shoes on the highest shelves for Tillar, had already intervened.

"What do you need, man? You want a custom dress? Some heels?" he asked in a serious tone as he climbed down the ladder, but the man still laughed like something was funny until Cam approached his little scrawny ass looking like the black Yao Ming. "Or better yet let me guess. You need directions back out that door before you find out this ain't about to go how you thought it would."

Country Bumpkin stood there for a second trying to prove that he wasn't intimidated by the human brick wall in front of him, but he was gone just as quickly as he had came in and I thanked Cam for helping me avoid catching another case.

"*He* needs to be thanking me. I know you keep that heat on you just waiting for a nigga to give you a reason," he joked about my concealed carry right as a very pregnant Tillar came waddling from our employee restroom. Faster than The Flash, he was at her side before I could blink twice and helping her back on the platform so that I could finish hemming her baby shower dress.

Before I had gotten to know him for myself I'd for real assumed that he was just love-bombing her with attention and affection those first six months they spent together in Chicago. But it had been way over a year now since he moved down here to Buckhead and that nigga really was just a fool for her, but the good kind. And after beating her brother's ass like he did and finally getting her away from her mean ass mama he had earned my respect for life.

But a small part of me was still worried that Cam might eventually turn out to be just like all other men. I had only met his two brothers once each, but there was no way that a fuckboy gene that strong hadn't hit him in some way no matter how good he had been at hiding it. And I knew with Tillar being in school and not working that he was footing the bill for everything because despite getting off to a good start with Thread we still weren't making a profit yet.

But while I considered myself to be the biggest, baddest feminist around these parts of Georgia, I also had the sense my mama gave me so I loved seeing black women being lavished and loved on. Of course I would never put myself in a situation to have to depend on a man upholding his word because they rarely did, but so far it was working out for Tillar and if he ever did try to switch up then she had me to rescue her because like always, one nigga didn't stop no show.

Saving her was the last thing on my mind currently though because she was back to getting on my last nerve fidgeting while I tried to fix her dress. Her feet hadn't gotten very swollen the whole pregnancy so she was still wearing heels regularly, but they had been looking like two loaves of bread the last couple weeks so I had to alter the length at the last minute.

"Tillar, if you don't stand the fuck still, I'm coming up there," I said through a pin in my mouth because she kept wiggling and messing up my new hemline.

"I'm trying, but I have to pee."

"You literally just peed before you got up here!"

"Well you try carrying a nine pound bag of baby on your bladder and see if you don't have to pee all the time too."

"No fucking thank you," I said as Cam helped her down again then smiled to myself as I watched her waddle back over to the bathroom.

Because of her height and build she was all belly and you almost couldn't even tell she was pregnant from behind. With my luck and short stature I would need a wheelbarrow to cart me around so I was never having kids. Besides I had paid too much to get good lasting work done on my body just to fuck it up for some no good nigga's big headed babies.

Bored and extra impatient now, I sighed while I walked over to the ceiling to floor mirrors that covered the walls across from the dressing rooms to get a look at myself. I already knew I still looked just as hit as when I left my condo that morning, but I hoped that my morning coffee had somehow improved something about my appearance.

It hadn't.

My unusually haggard looking mug and attire was due to the stress that came with planning an event that was supposed to be the talk of the city for a self-proclaimed bougie bitch like Tillar. Cam had given me financial carte blanche to do whatever I needed to throw her the baby shower of her dreams, but besides that and picking out a color palette neither of them had been much help.

I let it slide though because on top of preparing for my godson's birth in the next couple weeks they were also still getting moved into their new house and each taking classes. Tillar had one more semester to go until she was done with her fashion program and Cam had been taking a writing workshop because apparently he was writing a book about his family.

The whole thing sounded boring to me, but I wasn't much of a reader anyway. I would pick up the occasional graphic novel and of course I loved my manga and comics, but most people didn't consider those *real* reading so I guess I didn't either.

But in spite of my lack of event planning experience and complaining every step of the way, I had to pat myself on the back because I'd put together the perfect shower and I couldn't wait to see Tillar's face when she showed up. Sure her man may have paid for everything, but I worked so hard making sure that tomorrow went off without a hitch that I had already called dibs on the first pool party in their new courtyard.

I knew Tillar was about to hurry out of the bathroom when the beat to "F.I.L.A" by Scrappy started blasting throughout the store because that was always her get crunk song. And even though she was technically a transplant, I always let her rap her little heart out because I knew she meant every word as if she was born here and she really would love ATL forever.

I live for the A, I die for the A
I ride for the A so fuck what you say
What you know about I-20 to 285
Got a fine Atlanta bitch givin' head in the ride

And to think when we were first planning the vibe of the store, she had wanted to play nothing but boring jazzy elevator music. Even after being here so long, she still fell for the bougie façade that most natives put on, but we were gutter to our core because loving trap music was a southern pastime. I even temporarily ignored all the misogynistic lyrics because I didn't think I would ever be strong enough to resist shouting *Get on my level ho!*

She must've been feeling silly because she twerked on me for a minute and tried to get me out of my dry, funky mood.

"You better stop. That's how you got pregnant in the first place."

"No, I think that was reverse cowgirl," she said looking over at Cam who was on the phone and not paying us any attention. "I know you're tired of me asking, but you're really not gonna go to Tokyo?" she asked me once both of her wide feet were firmly planted on the platform again.

"I already told you I'm broke and I've seen every single *Hostel* movie and since you can't go with me then I'm not going," I said then reminded her that outside of *trust no nigga,* I only had one other rule and it was that I did not travel alone. If somebody ever wanted to snatch me up then they would have to come find me in the A.

"But you wouldn't even be in a hostel and that *Enchilada* manga man is paying for everything, right?" she asked butchering my favorite manga author's name and making me laugh in the process.

"Bitch, his name is Enji Oba and that's exactly how they get you to let your guard down.

Next thing you know I'll be sex trafficked in Tokyo and sucking dick for five hundred yen so I'mma keep my black ass in Georgia where it's safe."

"Okay, but why do all of your hypothetical scenarios end with you getting sex trafficked somewhere and sucking dick for the low?" she cracked on me and before I could give her a daily reminder of how that shit really did happen to women and girls every single day around the world, she beat me to speaking again.

"Plus that wouldn't even happen to you because you're practically a celebrity over there now. And I really hope you're not gonna let being scared to go by yourself keep you from something so big for you, Nic," she said sounding like I was disappointing her so I just decided not to say anything.

She wasn't exactly wrong about how major this thing would be, but for me my fears were much stronger than my desires sometimes and it certainly was in this case. And what was worse was that I couldn't even say that I had been waiting all my life for an opportunity like this because never in a million years did I think that *I* could become a reoccurring character in my favorite manga. Okay well not literally *me*, but a character using my likeness named Niko Ju so same difference.

The creator Oba claimed that he had been following me since I had first "gone viral" years ago when I attended Georgia Comic-Con as Storm from *X-Men*. But just between us, everybody really did overhype that look because it was just something that I had thrown together at the last minute, but after years of working in my family's tailoring shop the one thing I could do well was whip up something quick fast and in a hurry.

But more recently I had gotten Oba's attention when I did an online challenge where you had to dress up as every character in a manga and of course I chose his *Two Parts* because it was my favorite. The challenge was a fun but laid back thing that lots of people participated in but half-assed. I took it seriously though and put in work designing costumes and getting wigs and makeup looks together for weeks before I shared mine.

Lucky for me all the hype for the challenge had just about died down by the time my video was released, but it was worth the wait because it temporarily "broke the internet" and got me more followers than I could ever dream of. Oba even finally personally reached out and told me how much he enjoyed seeing his work handled with care and even praised my takes on his designs.

His initial intentions were to offer me a job as assistant costume designer for the upcoming live action movie, but by the time we had finished our video call he was practically begging me to let him create a character based on me too.

And of course I said yes because one of the rightful criticisms of the manga and anime was that it was majorly lacking in diversity when it came to female characters. Right off the bat I had made it crystal clear to him if he was going to draw me then I did not want to be white washed with straight hair or non-brown eyes. I wanted to look like myself. Whatever clothes he decided to draw me in were obviously up to him, but my look needed to be authentic because I would have loved to see somebody who looked like me in those old mangas that I hid from my mama under the floorboards in my closet.

I sighed when I realized that none of that would be happening at all because my scary ass had backed out the second he told me he wanted to fly me out for Tokyo's Comic-Con to go over everything.

Sensing that I was done with the subject Tillar decided to let me finish up her dress in peace, but she was obviously relieved when I told her I was done.

"About time. Baby C was really getting restless up here."

"Y'all still haven't come up with a name for that boy yet?" I asked a little irritated because weeks ago I had sworn I would go postal if I heard anybody else call that fetus Baby C again.

"Nope and Cameron *Junior* is still being stubborn about making him Cameron *the third*," she said throwing shade at Cam who was finally done finishing up the shelves so he smiled at her as he came back down.

"Well maybe that's because Cameron *Junior* just wants his son to have his own name and identity," Cam said, but she waved him off as he approached her.

"I guess, but Cameron Logan is a lucky name and I want my son to have it."

"You look really beautiful in this," he said cleverly changing the subject by focusing on the now finished dress and she fell for it by spinning around to let him see it from all angles.

"Thank you. Now can you help me get out of it before I have to go pee again?" she asked and I could tell that the sudden prospect of seeing her with it off came to his filthy mind by how he lifted her down from the platform and let her body slide down his.

"Hey leave that door open," I said after they began heading for the back room because I knew their freaky asses had gotten busy in there before. That's why I didn't even bother going to her bedroom anymore when I visited because she had put up mirrors everywhere when he first moved in and I knew exactly what that meant.

I'd skipped breakfast to get to the store on time that morning so right before my lunch hour swung around I was already looking at menus because I planned on ordering a big spread and pretending that I too was eating for two just like Tillar today.

After they were done in the back I had assumed that Cam would leave, but lately he had been sticking around when he could to do the few little tasks that Tillar was responsible for. So of course when a group of women came in for their appointment to pick out fabrics for bridesmaids dresses he naturally decided to play personal shopper to let Tillar put her swollen feet up and rest.

It was going normal at first, but there was always *one* in every group so it didn't surprise me when she decided to reveal herself to him. And she obviously hadn't bothered learning the meaning of subtlety because holding each fabric sample up to her full chest and asking Cam what he thought soon caught everybody's attention.

Well everybody except for Tillar who continued to flip through the latest issue of Vogue without a care in the world. I truly aspired to get to that level of being unbothered one day because my girl didn't even look up from the page when the woman forwardly asked Cam what his Valentine's Day plans were.

"Uh…I can't really say," he answered vaguely before the woman intrusively asked him why.

"Well my wife is sitting twenty feet away pretending like she's not listening to this conversation right now. And even though she told me she wanted me to take it easy this year, I still got a few tricks up my sleeve for her tonight and I want her to be surprised," he said knowing that would get Tillar's attention.

And he was right because he turned to smile at her the second she looked up at them. Ugh they could be so damn sickeningly sweet sometimes, but I welcomed it today because it was worth it getting to see the woman quickly decide to mind the business that paid her as she went looking for the bride.

"You really did get the last good one, huh?" I told Tillar after I had taken all of the women's measurements and placed an order for more of the chosen silky cerulean fabric that they'd all agreed on.

"Don't say that. You'll get one too," she said sympathetically in that Tillar way that I knew meant no harm even though it sounded like the same pity I felt for other women who were still foolishly waiting on men to get their shit together.

I guess it was just how we were brought up though because Tillar's daddy had raised her to be a princess meanwhile as much as Henry loved me, his only goal was to make sure I was wise enough to survive if something ever happened to him and Winnie because aside from them I didn't have anybody else. He had proudly taught me the game early and of course I lost a few times before falling in line and taking his advice to heart since everything he had warned me about with men came to fruition in one way or another.

"As usual you can save that 'good man' pep talk for somebody else because you already know they're 'bout as rare as hen's teeth," I said sounding just like Winnie's old country ass.

"Wassup Nic? We hating men again today?" Cam asked playfully after catching the tail end of our conversation.

"It's a day that ends in Y, right?" I asked and he just laughed because he knew it was true. I did like that he never seemed to take offense to anything since he knew he wasn't like the men I criticized. "Just do me a favor and raise this baby right so I can date him in twenty years," I joked as I rubbed Tillar's belly.

"Not happening. Besides there's already a full grown Logan with your name on him," he said casually before Tillar gave him a subtle gesture to zip his lips, but I had caught it.

"Wait what are you talking about?" I asked as I looked back and forth between them.

"Oh uh…I-I think I left my phone in the back so…yeah," he said then quickly left us alone out front.

I would've left the whole thing alone except the expression on Tillar's face when I looked up at her told it all. She knew but apparently wasn't going to say shit about it until I did.

"You know about the thing with me and Chase, don't you?" I asked her about our fling the weekend of her Halloween ball over a year ago and was met with a slow nod. "Why you ain't say something?"

"Well I thought you didn't want me to know so I've just been pretending like I didn't all this time," she reasoned as she leaned on the counter.

"How long is *all this time*? Since the ball?"

"No. Just since my wedding."

"Your wedding!" I damn near shouted at her because it was just as bad. "Tillar that's still over nine months ago."

"Tell me about it," she said as she touched her stomach. "Look it's no big deal. I know how private you are with that kind of stuff so we don't even have to talk about it."

"It's not that. It's just nothing to talk about."

"Yeah see that's what I figured," she said then tried to preoccupy herself with something mundane, but I wasn't letting her off that easily.

"So is he like talking shit about me or something? Is that how you found out?" I asked curiously because we hadn't exactly ended our extended one night stand on a high note.

"No. I mean I wouldn't know if he was. I just remember overhearing Reese telling Cam that she accidentally told Chris about it and--"

"Wait Reese and Chris know too?! Is there any-damn-body in that family who doesn't know my business?"

"Maybe their grandma?" she suggested. "But then again her interrogation skills are top notch so even that's not a guarantee."

"You know you big mouth Logans can't hold water for nothing."

"Obviously *I* can, but you should still come join us over here on the darkside. We have cake."

"Please, I would rather set my pussy hairs on fire before I ever let any man change my last name let alone Chase Logan."

"Well what exactly didn't you like about him?" she asked with that matchmaker gleam in her eyes that made me grunt loudly. "Okay okay. We're not talking about him. But now that you know I know, can I just ask one thing?" she asked right as the phone rang and I felt like I had been saved by the bell.

"Answer that for me," I told her as I walked over to the bathroom even though I had just been closer to it than she was. "All of your pissing today has finally rubbed off on me."

"Tills, you need me to get that?" Cam asked as he suddenly joined us again in the front of the store no doubt after eavesdropping.

"No, sweetie. I'm pregnant. Not handicapped. I can answer the phone by myself," she said before kissing his lips and picking it up. "Hello, thank you for calling Thread. This is Tillar speaking. How can I help you?"

I mouthed to her that I was "out" if it was for me before closing the door and finally getting a minute to myself. We hadn't even been too busy today, but I was already tired before I got here so every little thing was irritating me more than usual.

I sat there for longer than I needed just aimlessly scrolling my timeline until I heard what sounded like an intense whisper match going on between the two of them.

"Because she won't go alone anyway and it'll just drive her crazy until I can get up there with her!" I heard Tillar say.

"Not knowing is already driving her crazy. You heard what he said. She needs to get there before it's too late," Cam responded.

"No! I'm not telling her anything until we know for sure," she said before I flushed and washed my hands.

"What the hell are y'all out here fussing about?" I asked with a grin that I held until I saw it wasn't reciprocated by either of them.

"Nothing," Tillar said as she looked up and stared daggers into the side of Cam's face, but it didn't seem to bother him any.

"Yes something. That phone call was for you, Nic and it was somebody calling about your parents."

"Cam, I said no!" Tillar said angrily, but I didn't understand what all the hoopla was about because it was obviously a mistake.

"My parents? Who would be calling me here about them?" I asked before it dawned on me that he'd meant my birth parents not Winnie and Henry who had both passed years ago, Winnie from complications with Alzheimer's then Henry a couple months later from a broken heart.

I guess it made sense because I had finally bitten the bullet a few weeks ago and created a video about trying to find my birth parents. With all of the extra attention that I'd been getting on social media lately I figured that I would try to use those new eyes to help me get the answers I'd been looking for all of my life.

After sharing everything that I'd found out from private investigators over the years, I had hoped that somebody who knew the truth would reach out to me, but so far it was just other adoptees telling their stories and of course a few more opportunistic private investigators offering me their services. Well until now.

"Did they give names?" I asked Cam since Tillar had apparently planned on holding *this* water from me. I wasn't mad though because I knew from her words that her heart was in the right place and she was just trying to protect me.

"Yeah. Bernard and Angela Young from--"

"Rochester," we said simultaneously. "I know. That's where my mama Winnie's family is from. Angela is her baby sister," I said before asking what he'd meant when he said they needed to tell me before it was too late, but he let me know the call had ended before Tillar could find out why.

"Wait isn't Bernard your cousin BJ's first name? Are those his parents?" she asked and I nodded.

She only knew of him because I shared his music from time to time, but I hadn't actually seen him in person since we were kids. I was more than happy to support though because he was one of the few SoundCloud rappers with a buzz that made a point not to be disrespectful towards women with his lyrics.

"You think I should call first or wait until I get there? I should call, right? I shouldn't just show up," I said hurriedly while grabbing my purse from behind the register. I double checked that I had my IDs and debit card before requesting an Uber to the airport.

"Wait you're actually going by yourself? You won't go to Tokyo alone, but you'll go to ratchet ass Rochester?" she asked making me laugh for a second before I realized what she had just said. *I was going by myself.*

"Yeah you're not in any condition to fly and you won't be for a while so I have to do it on my own. This is what I've been waiting for," I said more to myself than anybody as I headed for the door, but she stopped me.

"Wait wait. I talked to Amber this morning and she said it's supposed to be a really bad storm tonight so her and Chris are just staying in for Valentine's Day," she said trying to warn me, but I just rolled my eyes at the mention of her new BFF Amber. Yeah I was jealous, and??

She hadn't stopped talking about her new *sister-in-law* and their babies since they had met a few months ago. Apparently this *Amber* was a follower on my feminist YouTube channel, but just like every other woman I knew she had fallen into the married with kids trap. I swear if that was what was in the cards for me then somebody would just have to reshuffle the deck.

"I'll be alright. If they're still flying out then it can't be too bad."

"But I don't want you to leave mad at me," Tillar said and I saw from the real tears welling in her eyes that she honestly thought I was upset about her not wanting to tell me about the call. I knew it was just the pregnancy hormones that had her more emotional than usual lately so I humored her.

"I promise I'm not mad about anything. You just promise not to be mad at me if I can't make it back in time for the shower tomorrow."

"Of course not," she said as she pulled me into a big hug. "You've done everything to make sure it was as special as possible for me and I really hope this works out for you. You deserve to finally know the truth."

"Thanks. And try not to have that baby before I get back here. Cross your legs, ho, and you," I said turning to Cam, "please don't open them," I told him as I saw my ride pulling up.

On the way to Hartsfield, I DMed BJ to give him my number and to ask him to call me as soon as possible. He followed instructions well because the second I got out of the car my phone was ringing in my hand. I quickly filled him in about the weird phone call, but he immediately knew I was telling the truth because he said that his mama Angela was being prepped for a double mastectomy today.

I could have dropped the phone right then and there from shock, but he assured me everything would be okay. Apparently she had beat cancer before so they were hopeful and prayed up about her doing it again. I instantly felt bad about not knowing much about that side of my family, but growing up Winnie had always kept me separated from them because they weren't Jehovah's Witnesses like her and Henry, at least that's what she had always told me.

I had to end the call while I bought my ticket for the next flight out, but I promised to call him right back when I got settled. I was pissed when I realized that there were no direct flights to Rochester so I would have to go to JFK in Queens and then drive six hours to get where I was going. Fuck my life.

"I could come pick you up if you want," BJ offered when I got him back on the line, but I declined because the flight was only a little over two hours and it just made more sense for me to drive myself. "So if what they said is true then that means you're my big sister?" he asked I guess after finally processing the full scope of things.

"I guess so. But can you do me a favor and not let them know I'm coming? I don't want to further stress anybody out in case I'm wrong about this."

"So why are you coming then if you think they got it wrong?"

"Because even if it's not true, I bet they know something so I'm gonna make them tell me."

"Alright well I'll be looking out for you cuz. Or sis. Damn. This is all kinds of fucked up," he said laughing nervously.

"I know. Just don't say anything," I repeated before I put my phone up.

I had to pull it right back out though when I remembered that I would need a car to get me to Rochester. I googled rental places near the airport, but every one that I called said that they would be closing soon because of the storm. That's when it hit me that I had left Thread without grabbing a light jacket let alone an actual winter coat.

I sighed because even though this clearly wasn't gonna be easy, I was still going. I would just have to figure the rest out when I got there.

♛

I was born with a head full of hair so people had been calling me Rapunzel all of my life, but I really only got annoyed with all of these inches on two occasions, wash day and when I went to the airport. Nobody who knew me ever made a fuss about it anymore, but there was nothing like catching a last minute flight to remind me that having so much hair was unusual.

It wasn't uncommon at all to see a thirty inch weave walking around these days, but I guess the fullness of the fifty inches sprouting from my scalp just looked overwhelming on my barely five feet tall ass. It'd been wrapped up in a messy braided bun all day, but sure enough TSA made me undo it all to prove that I wasn't hiding anything in there.

I was always understanding about that part, but I really didn't appreciate how they would stick their fingers in it to make sure it was real because it always made me feel dirty. I would just have to deal with it today though because I had more important shit to worry about.

It had to be at least twenty years since I had been to Rochester for a family reunion back in the day and ironically or maybe not now, that was the event where I found out that I was adopted. I was ten years old at the time and I'd never had any inkling that my mama and daddy weren't actually my mama and daddy. I had the same rich cocoa colored skin as both of them and people always told me that I was Henry's twin, but I guess it was true what the old folks said: if you fed them long enough they would start to look like you and trust they did a helluva lot more than just feed me.

But anyway when I overheard a group of cousins and aunties saying how it was such a shame that Winnie would never have any kids of her own while watching me play, I immediately knew what was up. I was a big girl so I didn't even cry when I asked her about what they had said, but I fell the fuck out when she told me that we were leaving because I was having such a good time playing with all my cousins including BJ who I had just met for the first time.

On the long drive back to Georgia they finally decided to tell me the truth, or at least part of it. Winnie said that a nice young woman from Kingdom Hall had found herself "in trouble" and they decided to raise me since she couldn't. I believed the simple explanation then because I figured they wouldn't lie to me twice. And by then I knew how babies were made so I was relieved that they hadn't done *that* to make me. But after the relief I was left wondering about the people who actually *had* made me and why they didn't want to keep me.

And listen I'd had a great home by most peoples' standards and I swear I wouldn't trade my folks for anything in this world, but I honestly wished that I had never found out because I wouldn't wish the type of mental longing that came from feeling abandoned on anybody, not even the niggas I hated the most.

No matter what I could never sleep on planes so I usually just rested my eyes until I landed, but all of the memories and theories running through my mind had somehow made me doze off for a while and when I opened them we were flying over New York. From above the ground looked like the North Pole, completely white and covered in a thick blanket of snow, but unfortunately where I was headed wouldn't be filled with Christmas cheer.

I didn't have anything with me but my purse so when it was time to get off the plane, I was the first one out. I didn't know what I was in a hurry for though because I still didn't know where I was gonna get a car or a ride from. I contemplated Uber hopping until I got there, but I had just paid rent and for this damn flight so my bank account was looking pretty sad at the moment. But instead of worrying Tillar with those details, I just let her know that I had made it safely and that I was about to start the drive. And speaking of Tillar...

What would she do if she was here in my shoes?

I thought about that for a minute before realizing that she wouldn't have even been in this situation because Cam would've already had several contingency plans to make sure everything went right for her. I smiled at the thought then grimaced at the idea that popped into my head next because it involved calling imitation Cam also known as Chase since he was the next best thing and just so happened to live in New York.

I knew that I could have sent out a message on social media and had several thirsty men offering to pull up for me, but at a time like this I just wanted to feel safe and be with somebody that I was at least a little bit familiar with. And in spite of how badly we had left things after the last time we talked, I knew that he would look out for me if I swallowed my pride and asked for his help.

I didn't have his number, but it didn't matter because I wasn't in the mood to talk anyway so I decided to DM him on his official Instagram account even though I was aware of at least one fake page that he had been following me on too. And I swear I didn't even know why this man was so obsessed with me because I was a proud Pillow Princess with him. I mean why should I have to work up a sweat and get tired just to get a nut when I could make men like him do all of the work?

I wasn't auditioning to be some nigga's wife so no I wasn't riding dick from here to Timbuktu and no I wasn't deep-throating until I was hoarse. Hell he would be lucky if I decided to roc the mic period because I was selective about that too. I needed to see recent results and I did a visual inspection before I put my mouth on anything.

"Chase, I know it's been a minute since we last talked but I'm in New York and I need help and I don't know anybody else up here."

I hurried and sent the message before I vomited on myself because I hated how damsel-ly I had to make it sound, but I'd only done it because I knew deep down men loved that shit. As much as they tried to escape being responsible, nothing got their dicks harder than knowing there was a woman somewhere who needed them.

And I was shameless in using that to my benefit when I felt like it because any man who I dealt with knew the deal out the gate. They were blocked in my phone until I needed a favor or sex or both because I refused to be bombarded with *Good morning* texts and empty promises just to get what I wanted. And if by chance one thought too highly of himself and said no then he was blocked and deleted forever then on to the next.

Lucky for me though I already knew that Chase wouldn't be able to stop himself from helping me so I didn't even bother sitting on the edge of my seat while I waited. And I was right not to because a minute later I saw those three dots telling me that not only had he seen my message, but that he was responding to it. But if I was being honest, my heartbeat did go a little faster when I saw him start then stop typing a few times before finally just asking me what I needed.

"I know it's a lot to ask but can I borrow your car until tomorrow?"

"Oh and a coat too?" I added when those frigid New York winds disrespectfully slapped me across the face yet again.

Instead of answering either of my questions he just asked where I needed to be picked up from, but I suggested getting an Uber to where he was to avoid having to drop him back off. He hesitated again for a minute before finally sending me his location.

Well that was easy, I thought as I blew on my fingers and waited for my ride to show up. A little too easy might I add, but I had no time to look a gift horse in the mouth or even really think about what I was getting myself into because it was working out. Yeah the weather wasn't the best, but I would get the car and drive very slowly and maybe get to Rochester around midnight. Then after seeing what was going on up there I would return the car and make it home just in time for Tillar's baby shower tomorrow.

Despite the weather being so bad I made it

to Chase a minute before the Uber had estimated which was a minute too long because I was not looking forward to facing the cold again. I didn't have to worry about that though because right after getting out I saw him coming down the steps of a nice brownstone on the other side of the street.

He nodded when he saw me then waited for a couple cars to pass before walking over. I had forgotten just how tall he was until he was standing over me and putting a big, long men's coat in my hands.

"Hey. Thank you so much for this," I said genuinely because like I'd said it was a lot to ask for. He didn't bother saying *You're welcome* though and just looked at me like he was expecting something else.

"Aren't you gonna put it on?" he finally asked about the coat.

"Yeah after I pee. Can I use your bathroom?" I asked as I crossed one leg over the other. I'd had to go since I landed, but I only used public bathrooms when there were no other options.

"Hold it," he said rudely like I didn't look like I would blow any second. "I have to make a stop before I give you the keys. You can go there," he said adjusting his tone, but now I was the one who was about to come off ill-mannered.

"Well how long is that gonna take because I

don't have a lot of time."

"You don't have a lot of stuff today, huh?" he asked with a little too much snark for my liking as he opened his passenger door for me. I was expecting a Prius or something completely electric by how he was always talking about gardening and recycling on Instagram, but it was one of those old school cars.

"What is that supposed to mean?"

"You don't have a car, a coat or patience," he said matter-of-factly, but instead of arguing back I just got in.

"Whatever. Just try to make it quick."

Thankfully he'd already had the car running and it was warmed and ready to go with the heat on full blast so that helped me feel a little less like I was about to burst.

"What's that smell?" I asked him even though I didn't want to say too much to him, but I couldn't ignore that scrumptious scent coming from the backseat if I had tried to.

"Soup."

"It smells really good."

"Well I can cook so..." he said sounding like he was irritated, but I couldn't tell if it was because of the bad driver from the car in front of us or me.

"Hey you still live with that girl, don't you?" I asked him when I realized that he had given me the wrong address for the Uber because I'd seen him coming out of the building across the street where he actually lived.

"She moved out today," he said simply then didn't bother to offer any further explanation. I didn't need it anyway, but I had to dig a little because nobody broke up on holidays unless there was something foul going on.

"On Valentine's Day? Damn you must've really fucked up because most women would have at least stuck it out for the gift."

"I didn't fuck anything up," he said sounding defensive but still not very convincing.

"So then why did she dump you?"

"How do you know that I didn't break up with her?" he asked as he momentarily took his eyes off the road to put them on me, but I just smacked my lips.

"Why did she dump you, Chase?" I repeated before he focused again and put his hands at ten and two.

"She thought there was somebody else, but it wasn't," he swore, but I just had a good laugh as I felt my fingers finally getting toasty from holding them by the heat vent. "What's so funny?"

"Nothing. Just that y'all will lie with a straight face on your deathbeds about shit women already know."

"But I'm not lying. I didn't cheat," he said definitively which practically forced me to bring up what I had sworn I wouldn't.

"Okay so what do you call what you did with me then?" I asked sarcastically which caused him to grip the steering wheel tighter.

"A mistake," he said with his voice suddenly sounding as icy as the streets we were driving on and if I weren't already defrosting I would have taken a chill. I wouldn't let him see that though.

"Mm one time is a mistake. Two times is a choice."

"No. Two times is *two mistakes* and I haven't made that mistake since."

"Oh so you must be one of those opportunistic cheaters then? You know in general you're a decent dude until your girl is out of town or you go to a bachelor party, right?" I asked playfully, but all I got was a hard sigh in response.

"Like I said, I'm not a cheater, Nicole," he repeated in a tone that let me know he wasn't interested in continuing with this subject so I dropped it altogether. His ass was still a cheater though.

Still having to pee really badly, I immediately went to get out of the car when we arrived at our destination, but he quickly said he would get the door for me. It wasn't until he'd opened it that we realized my long braid had gotten stuck in it and my ends were covered in dirty snow from dragging in the street.

I sighed and cleaned off what I could as he offered up a lame *My bad*. For the past week all I had been wanting was a good deep cleaning and condition, but I had been holding off because of the baby shower and I didn't have the energy to wrestle with my head. Now I would definitely have to do it as soon as I got home.

One look at the sign on the front of the building we pulled up to let me know that it was some sort of luxury assisted living place for the elderly. It didn't take long for me to figure out that he was there to drop off soup to the grandma that Cam was always talking about. It instantly made me thankful that Winnie and Henry were pretty self-sufficient while they were still here because no matter how nice it was I could never see myself putting them in a place like this.

"You're really bringing soup to your sick grandmother? What are you, *Little Red Riding Hood*?"

"That's funny. I'm the only one who knows how to make it just like she does so we're gonna stay in and watch her favorite movies tonight."

"That's nice of you," I told him, but I was lying because I had always believed that the only thing worse than a mama's boy was a grandmama's boy.

One quiet and awkward ride up an elevator later and he was letting himself into a unit and me into the bathroom near the door. I rushed in and made it just in time because a minute later and I would have been pissed *and* pissy.

"Gram, are you dressed? I have somebody here with me for a minute," he yelled to the back of the small but fancy apartment.

The sweet old lady voice that I was familiar with sounded strained as she answered and asked him to bring her a robe from her room before whispering and asking who the hell he had brought over while she wasn't feeling well. I laughed to myself because it seemed like nobody but me could actually whisper these days.

"It's just a friend and she'll be leaving right after using the bathroom," he explained, but she scoffed.

"She? Chasen Anthony, I know you move fast, but you just got rid of Parker today. Don't tell me you already have another one," she said in a tone that reminded me of Winnie back when I used to have a new crush every week.

"It's not like that. I'm just letting her borrow the Bluebird while I stay with you tonight," he said then stopped talking when I entered the living area where they were seated.

"Oh it's just you, Nicole," she said sounding relieved that it was me and not a complete stranger. This was only our third time meeting, but I guess that counted for something to her.

"You remember her from the ball, Gram?" he asked confused about how familiar we actually were.

"Well I'm old not senile. And if you had bothered to attend Cameron's wedding then you would have known that I spent quite some time with Nicole then as well," she said with a wink reminding me of the Long Island iced tea I had snuck up to her room after Cam wouldn't let her have any drinks because of her medication. "I tell you these boys and their sibling rivalry will be the death of me."

"I hope not, Miss Ida. It's so nice to see you again, ma'am. And I'm sorry to barge in on your movie night with Chase. I just hate all public restrooms but especially those little bitty ones on planes," I said honestly even though I had gotten over my discomfort enough to join the mile high club once before.

"Oh it's no problem, honey. You'll just have to excuse my appearance because I'm a bit under the weather."

"Are you kidding me? You look just fine," I said as I looked her over because she looked tired but comfy in her jammies and robe. "You don't even want to see me when I'm sick. I'm perfectly healthy now and I look like I got hit by a

Greyhound bus," I joked as I looked down at myself.

"Well let's just try to remember how beautiful we looked on other occasions and forget this one ever happened," she warmly chuckled out and it brought a smile to my face.

"Will do," I said before noticing Chase watching me and looking uncomfortable at the whole situation.

"Are you ready to go now?" he asked me before fishing out his keys and I nodded. "Alright the tank is full, but the Bluebird doesn't hold gas like it used to so you should probably stop when you're about halfway there and coming back."

"And just where are you driving to in this storm if you don't mind me asking?" Ida asked me with a bit of a dry cough.

"It's a long story, but I've got a family emergency up in Rochester."

"Oh I'm sorry to hear that, but Rochester is an awful long way to be going by yourself. Do you know where you're going, honey?"

"Not really, but the gps will get me there in no time."

"Oh no. We can't have your little self all alone on these roads," she said like we weren't around the same size and height. "It's settled. Chase you're going with her," she said definitively as she turned to him, but the frown on his face said otherwise.

"Gram, I can't go. You know I have to stay here and take care of you."

"I'll be just fine. I've got my soup now and I would much rather watch my Billy Dee movies alone. Besides I think Nicole needs you more than I do tonight," she said sternly all of a sudden.

"But she doesn't even want me to go. Do you?" he asked looking up at me from his seated position.

"Well…" I began to say no but decided to let him know that I wasn't exactly sure if I would be comfortable driving after all because I already had a hard time reaching some newer pedals and the ones in his old car seemed even farther down.

He didn't even bother to let me finish. He just sighed hard then stood to his feet. Usually I would have said nevermind to everything, but I tucked my pride in tightly because beggars couldn't be choosers and I would have gladly dealt with his attitude if it meant me making it there and back safely.

"Alright now drive safely and call me when you get there. I don't care how late it is," Ida told him after he had bundled her up on the sofa with her soup and then kissed her forehead.

"I will. Get some rest and I'll be back in the morning."

"Seems like you have a Valentine now after

all," she half-whispered to him on my way out and I outwardly cringed because I really couldn't catch a break. Tillar had been right. Even his damn grandma knew I'd fucked him the first night I met him.

I was about to ask him about how she knew, but just as we were stepping back out into the cold, I almost slipped on a sneaky piece of ice. Luckily he was right behind me and caught me before I hit the pavement because that would have been a downer.

"Be careful. Your shoes have no grip," he said about the little slip-ons that were on my feet.

"Yeah we don't get much snow down in Atlanta."

"I know. Cam told me about how the whole city acted over those two inches y'all got last winter," he said sounding amused for a second before getting stern just like Ida all of a sudden. "Look it's getting pretty bad out here. Why don't you just get a room for the night and then I can take you tomorrow?"

A misty cloud formed in front of me from my winter breath as I sighed because men were always trying to dictate how shit should go. And he was probably just trying to see if I was stupid enough to let him make another "mistake" with me now that he was really alone on Valentine's Day.

"I already told you it's an emergency so I don't have until tomorrow. If you don't want to go or if you changed your mind about loaning me the car, just let me know now so I can figure out another way to get there," I said stubbornly while looking down at my phone to get the point across that I would be getting to Rochester with or without him.

"No. I just told my Gram I would get you there so I will. She would kill me if something happened to you and I refuse to let you be the cause of my death," he said coldly, but it didn't match his actions because he held onto my arm as he carefully walked me over to the car and opened the door. "Is all of you in this time?" he asked looking down at my hair with a slight smile that I tried and failed not to return.

"Looks like it."

"Alright then. We can go," he said before hurrying around to get inside and warm the car up again. "Before we get on the road, are you hungry? I saw the way you looked when you smelled that soup."

"Um…yeah I guess I could eat," I told him when I realized how my hunger was also contributing to that worried feeling in my stomach because I had left town before I could have lunch.

"There's not much open because of the

storm, but I could whip up something because my restaurant is right down the street. Plus since we're making this a road trip, we'll need some road snacks. I'm not touching anything that I didn't make from here to upstate," he joked, but it reminded me about how critical he had been about room service the last time we were together.

*"Of course I don't expect it to be as good as **my** food, but the least they could do is make it fresh. I'm not eating this."*

He wasn't wrong about the restaurant being so close either because I felt like we had barely gotten warm before we were getting out again in front of Blaze. I wanted to be a hater and act like it wasn't impressive, but even I had to admit that his spot was nice and bigger than I expected it to be. Or maybe it just looked different due to the emptiness. Either way I had never known a chef or somebody who owned a restaurant before so I slowly took it all in.

I assumed that I would just wait in the dining area while he cooked, but he insisted I come to the back while he did his chef shit. I wasn't interested in seeing him trying to show off for me, but I did decide to go along as a precaution to make sure he didn't roofie anything.

See being aware of men's true nature and how much pain and destruction they brought to the world was really eye opening when Henry taught me about it, but it was sad too because it made me start questioning every man I came across and wondering what dark thoughts he was really thinking about when he saw me. I tried to push that to the back of my mind for now though because even I didn't have the energy for it today. I was just gonna have to trust this fool and hope for the best.

"What are you making?" I asked after he was done washing his hands and pulling out a bunch of vegetables.

"Well first I'm gonna make some stuff like poke that's best served cold for the road then something hot for now."

"Poke? You know some luncheon meat and white bread won't hurt you just this once, right?" I asked seriously, but he laughed like I was playing.

"How about you grab an apron and be my prep cook? That way we can get out of here faster and you can have a say in what we make, but I can tell you now it won't be lunch meat," he remarked lightheartedly and I noted that being in the kitchen seemed to put him in a better mood.

I wanted to say no, but I couldn't exactly object to anything that would help me get closer to answering questions I'd been asking myself since I left home that morning.

"You're doing that wrong," he said after I had literally chopped off two slices of a carrot.

"What, you want me to *julienne* them or something, Rachel Ray?"

"No, just not what you're doing now. Here let me help," he said before putting his knife down and coming up behind me to guide my hands. I ignored the electric shock I felt when his body faintly pressed into mine then let him show me how to do it his way.

"It's all in the wrist and you don't have to pick the knife up each time. Just rock it back and forth to get a diagonal cut like this. See how much better that looks?" he asked with his head bent and his mouth much too close to my ear for me to coherently answer so I just slipped away from his grasp.

"I'm probably gonna slow you down so I think I'mma just watch," I told him and he nodded as he got back to work. He did still explain everything he was doing as he went, but it was too fast for me to pick up on. For whatever reason I didn't let him know that though and I just pretended to be engaged in what he was saying.

I did interrupt him for a second when my phone went off in my hand and I realized that I didn't have a charger with me. The battery was still halfway full from this morning, but I knew it wouldn't last until tomorrow. He told me that he would let me use the charger he kept in the car as he finished packing up a little cooler with fancy looking acai and poke bowls and some kind of cold soup that I knew I wouldn't be eating.

He ended up making a few sandwiches after all, but they were gourmet and looked nothing like the cold cuts I had grown up on. I had nothing but good memories though of me and Henry slamming that old-fashioned loaf for dinner whenever Winnie didn't feel like cooking.

By the time he was done searing two steaks and cooking a "medley of vegetables" or whatever it was that he had described, I was getting impatient so I just decided to ask him about the picture I had seen on the way in. It was of him and LeBron James standing in front of the restaurant pointing up at the sign.

"When did that happen?" I asked as I sat on my hands before I started ringing them and showing signs of my impatience at how long he was taking with his little pan sauce.

"A few months ago after he beat the Nets. I cooked for his manager's wedding a few years ago and he's liked my food ever since," he said casually even though I could tell he was proud of that fact.

"That's cool. You know I'm surprised none of you big Logan boys played ball. Y'all are all just a waste of height."

"Actually I used to play in high school and I was pretty good, but Chris and Cam can't ball for shit."

"Well what made you quit and start cooking then?"

"I knew I would never be as good as the best," he said as he pointed up at LeBron, "and I like being the best at whatever I do."

"But Bron isn't the best. Maybe top five if I'm feeling nice," I said before letting him know that I wasn't just a casual watcher. Henry had always loved it so after a while I began studying the game and grew to love it too.

"If he's not the best then who is and you better not say Jordan? I'll even give you Kobe, but if you say Jordan you're not getting any dessert," he joked as he meticulously spooned sauce on the plates.

"My nigga. Jordan has six rings. *Six*. Let me know when your boy catches up…if he ever does," I said with plenty of shade as I sipped the bottle of water he had given me.

"But it's not just about rings. If it was just about rings then Bill Russell would be the goat and we both know them niggas wasn't really balling out like that in the sixties."

"Spoken like a clueless man. Championships and rings literally mean everything."

"Maybe to most people, but for me it's about the way they play the game and there's nobody better than or who's done more for the sport than King James," he said with so much conviction that I just rolled my eyes and let him have it.

Usually I would have laid out my case and crushed all of his dick riding with an actual and factual PowerPoint presentation that I kept in my email, but I decided to forgo that and try to be nice to him because I needed him. This was why I didn't like needing them.

"Hey I don't mean to be rude, but can you hurry up with that? It's dark and we really need to get going."

"Here it comes. Good food takes time," he said as he finally put a plate in front of me.

"Well I already told you I don't have a lot of time."

"Yeah that's about all you've told me. When are you gonna tell me why we're going to Rochester?" he asked as he took the seat next to me with a plate of his own.

"I'm not because it's complicated and none of your business," I told him straightforwardly, but he said he wasn't gonna let me slide with that. "Alright whatever. I was told if I wanted to meet my birth parents to come to Rochester before it's too late."

"And who told you this?"

"I don't know. Probably a distant cousin or somebody who saw my YouTube video a few weeks ago."

"So that's all you know? What if it's a serial killer luring you up there?"

"Then I'm gonna die regretting spending my last day with you," I said sarcastically and he smiled.

"You like it?" he asked after I had finally taken a bite of the steak and veggies. It was well seasoned and undeniably tender and that sauce was what dreams were made of so I nodded, but I refused to verbalize it because I knew he wanted me to.

"Where did the name Blaze come from?"

"You really want to know?" he asked as he sat his fork and knife down.

"I asked, didn't I?"

"Okay so there was this girl, well woman, named Blaze who used to work at a strip club in DC back when I was at Howard and uh…let's just say I've never seen a split like that in my life," he said obviously reminiscing on whatever nasty things he had done with her. "Anyway I randomly ran into her while I was planning the menu for this place and it just made sense."

"You know I really can't believe you're Cam's brother," I said giving him a stank face, but he thought it was funny.

"You know he's really not as perfect as everybody thinks he is, right?" he said and even though he wasn't heavy-handed with it in his food, the saltiness was finally coming out of him.

"You should already know by now that I don't think any man is perfect," I told him while unintentionally looking into his eyes and a strange silence followed before he tried to lighten up the vibe again.

"Okay where did the name Thread come from since you think you're an expert at choosing names?"

"Definitely not from a stripper," I said making him laugh, but seeing his smile bothered me and made me want to bring up the elephant in the room before I got too comfortable. "Chase, why did you tell your whole family that we slept together?"

He didn't seem caught off guard by the accusation, but he did immediately put his defenses up.

"I didn't tell anybody anything about us. My cousin Reese saw me leaving your hotel room and it didn't take a rocket scientist to know what we were doing in there," he rationally explained before letting his bitterness overtake the aforementioned saltiness. "And you and I both know I planned on never speaking to you again after what you said to me so I definitely wouldn't be telling niggas about us."

"Refresh my memory," I said trying to hold in a laugh because I knew exactly what I'd said to cut him so deeply. "What did I say that was so bad? Because I thought I actually let you down pretty easily because you were Cam's brother."

"You don't really believe that, do you?"

"Yeah. And I'm just trying to imagine what you wanted me to say? What, I was supposed to risk it all for some cheating ass nigga in a Jheri curl wig?" I asked thinking back on his *Pulp Fiction* Halloween costume.

"No, you were supposed to risk it all for the nigga that made your toes curl up and your eyes roll in the back of your head," he said smugly like that was some big accomplishment.

"That's cute. You really think you're the first dude that made my toes curl?" I asked then didn't even bother holding in my laugh anymore when it became evident that he really did think that. It only seemed to make him angry though, I noted as he narrowed his eyes at me.

"No *FreakNic*, I bet I wasn't the first," he said harshly and as much as I hated to admit it, hearing him call me that dumb name shut me up real quick. "But what we did wasn't just some regular one night thing and you know it. You felt that shit too."

"Felt what?" I asked as I picked my

shoulders back up, trying to physically recover from that verbal blow he had just sent my way.

"That spark," he said sounding like a bad cliché.

"Chase, stop it with that goofy shit. There was not no damn spark between us," I vehemently denied, but he openly disagreed until I spoke over him. "And even if it was, I don't do sparks. They're dangerous and more often than not lead to dumb decisions like trying to convince a complete stranger who lives hundreds of miles away to be your girlfriend even though you already have one," I told him matter-of-factly and *that* shut him up.

"Sparks" or rather the idea of sparks worked for who it worked for, people like Tillar and Cam, but they would never be for me because you had to control them motherfuckers or else they could start the kind of fires that couldn't be contained. And just like my hair, I couldn't, no I *wouldn't* be tamed.

2

TRAP HOUSE

CHASE

I knew all the shit that people said about me, but trust me almost none of it was true. What was true was that my grandmother, better known as Gram had babied my youngest brother Chris and that my oldest brother Cam was always up under our dad so that left me with my fair share of middle child syndrome.

This wasn't *The Brady Bunch* though so I wasn't going out like Jan. I started working on my dad's car, The Bluebird, with him and Cam after school and I would have just enough time to wash my hands to help Gram and Chris start dinner. Basically I had to get in where I fit in because they were the only parents I had. My mother Carolyn had died a month before I turned one while giving birth to Chris. And I guess that whole thing was why I wasn't too interested in having kids of my own, but that wasn't important for now.

Being a year apart with both Cam and Chris

put me in a unique position. I had a connection with them both that they were missing with each other because I was simultaneously little brother and big brother. But from the very beginning it was always me and Chris against the world and it had stayed that way up until recently when he'd gotten married and had a baby with his wife Amber.

Now don't get me wrong, I loved my niece and I was glad she was born, but babies just had a way of changing people in a way that I never wanted to be changed. AJ had only been in the world a couple months, but already the new responsibilities that came with her had caused a rift between me and Chris while bringing him closer with Cam who was also expecting a baby boy with his wife Tillar.

Now that wouldn't have been so bad if it didn't coincide with the decline on my relationship with Cam. We had never been super close, but we had formed a temporary alliance to get Chris on board with selling our dad's house since he had been passed for two years now, but Cam switched up on me at the last minute and made me look like the bad guy.

But if I was being real I had started seeing a change in my relationship with Chris long before that when he had collapsed from exhaustion at work last year. Yeah I wasn't there for him when he got out of the hospital like I probably should've been, but I had a restaurant to run and I wasn't going to sacrifice my business when the old Chris wouldn't have done it for me. He would have just said *That's what your bitch is for* and kept it pushing.

It probably didn't help either that I didn't know just how serious shit had gotten with him and Amber until after this past Thanksgiving when we all found out she was pregnant. But it was because he had just said that she'd left that summer and never mentioned her to me again. Of course before they got married he confessed everything, but by then it was too late especially since he even told Cam before me. That was the ultimate violation because we had told each other everything since we could talk, but now I didn't feel like I knew him anymore.

And because of that I felt like I didn't even have brothers anymore because Cam had violated me years before Chris did when he just up and left after his daughter Cree and his wife Summer were killed. I understood that his hurt was on another level than the rest of the family, but they both meant something to us too and I was hurt that he didn't let us grieve with him.

I was the first one at the hospital when it happened and every now and then I sat back and wished that I would have stayed in the car just a little while longer, at least until somebody who was better equipped could have helped me deal with what I saw. My big brother was covered in his kid's blood crying his soul out on the white hospital floor because his only child was gone and there was nothing that he could do about it.

But as heartbreaking as that was, it was just the beginning. For weeks he barely said a word, but the tears never stopped coming. He cried an ocean's worth and lost mad weight from not eating even though I had started bringing him special made dinners every night from my first restaurant. Then out of nowhere I stopped by with his food one night and he was just gone.

And yeah what had happened was fucked up but just leaving everybody behind without a word was another level of fucked up. If it wasn't for Reese calling to let us know that he was with her in Chicago, we would have thought he was dead too. I had sworn that I would never forgive him for the way he worried Gram and my dad those few days, but I eventually let that shit go because I didn't know what I would've done in that situation.

What was unforgivable though was how he had acted when we found out a few years later that my dad was fatally ill. He called to talk to him every day but never once came to hospice to visit because he claimed that he didn't want to see him like that. It was a cop out though because me and Chris didn't want to see him like that either, but we were both still there as much as we could be, me so much that the restaurant I was running then, my third Full Plate, suffered and ended up having to close. It was already headed in that direction anyway, but taking on so much with my dad definitely helped it close a lot faster so it was fuck Cam forever.

But I didn't have time to be worrying about my lack of a relationship with my brothers lately. I was now on my fourth restaurant, my baby Blaze, and I wasn't letting anything get in the way of it succeeding. I was proud to finally be able to have a farm-to-table style restaurant and the only outsourced item I served was the fresh bread that was delivered daily from the bakery down the block.

We were most known for our bougie hipster brunch menu and strong mimosas because I was a proud member of the day party and rooftop crowd in Brooklyn, but our dinner menu could compete with the best of the best with or without a Michelin star. It hadn't gone unnoticed either because after making some important culinary lists, I'd been approached by an investor about "bringing Brooklyn to the south". He first wanted to franchise Blaze and put it in key southern cities like Memphis, Charleston, and Atlanta before eventually going nationwide.

At first it sounded too good to be true and I had to pinch myself after every meeting, but it was really happening and it had only taken three failed restaurants and a badly bruised chef ego to get here. And to think right before opening Blaze I had almost listened to a few friends of mine from culinary school that advised me to go back and work underneath more established chefs for a while before trying to do my own thing again.

I'd mulled it over for a few months, but I always knew I would never be able to work under anybody again because I was too bullheaded to *Yes Chef* another man to death. That's why I jumped in head first and opened my first restaurant Logan at just twenty-four. Of course it failed, but I had learned a lot and applied it to my second Eden. That one failed too, but it was in no way indicative of my skills as a chef because everybody knew that a successful restaurant was about more than just good food. The timing had to be right too, but I lacked patience back then because I liked to do things my way.

I was classically trained, but I only pulled out that shit to keep my skills sharp and up to date or to show off sometimes. It was cliché, but real cooking was about putting your heart and soul in your food. I watched how my Gram always picked greens with care because she knew that they would eventually end up on somebody's plate. Reflecting on that was what eventually taught me patience because sure whipping up something quick was a skill within itself, but the good stuff took time and it was always worth the wait.

After so many back-to-back failures though, I had contemplated giving up chef life altogether because working in a restaurant was hard. But I just didn't want to have wasted all that time I'd spent getting to where I was now because I knew more than anything that would have disappointed my dad who had always told me to never quit on myself.

That was easier said than done though because trying to always be professional in the face of racist ass kitchen staffs in competitive environments with low wages could break anybody. That and the fact that I wanted to be a trailblazer in this field was why I eventually had to separate from the mindset of a traditional trained chef. Because while the techniques and shit was important, it wasn't what made the food I grew up eating good. It was cooking it with Gram or my dad and my brothers, the family aspect and the love.

That's why this time around I made sure to not just hire the best people for the job. I wanted to love and respect everybody on my team and show it by paying them livable wages. That hurt business some too, but I knew what it was like working seventy hours a week but still not having enough for rent and health insurance. Luckily I'd had a well off family and a trust to fall back on when I was doing it, but everybody else wasn't as fortunate as me.

And one more thing people probably never thought about was that working in a kitchen was hot as fuck. I didn't know if it was because I was bigger than most people at six-six, but even stepping into the freezer for a quick break barely cooled me down sometimes so I'd decided early on in my career that if I was going to be sweating then it would be in my own shit.

Yeah I was young and arrogant then and I just knew I cooked the best food in the world. Not much had changed over the years except that I had gotten a little older and I wasn't chasing Michelin stars anymore. It would've been wasted energy anyway because the industry only accepted ass kissing chefs that looked like me and the only ass I kissed was on the woman who laid next to me at night.

Parker was somebody that had been in the background of my life for years. We ran in the same circles so we were both known to be friendly and flirty, but it was never the right time because she was always in a relationship or I was in one. Finally the stars aligned in our favor a few years ago and we decided to give us a real shot. And there was no question that it was the best situation I'd ever been in and that was saying something because I had been collecting girlfriends since I stopped collecting Pokémon cards.

Loving her as much as I did had even made me create a bond with her ten year old son Nathan. See dating women with kids was never a dealbreaker for me like it was with Chris because I always knew that I didn't want any of my own. But if I did ever one day decide to have a son I would want him to be just like Nate because he was a good kid.

And I wouldn't lie and act like I "loved" him like he was my own because I didn't, but I cared about him a lot. Our relationship was more like big brother and little brother and he was even starting to kick my ass in NBA2K in a way that made me proud, but as a rule I never disciplined him. I just supported Parker however I could when I was home, not that I was much because running a restaurant took time. Time that was supposed to be used to have a life and take my relationship with her to the next level, but like I had said my time was only for finally becoming a success.

We had been at a standstill for a while now anyway, but we were both holding on for different reasons. She didn't want another failed relationship and I felt like I would be letting everybody down by not being with her. She had been in an abusive relationship before me so I had taken it upon myself to save her and Nathan from it since I had seen how bad things like that could get with Cam, Summer and Cree.

But it was looking like I didn't have a say in whether we stayed together or not now because she had finally reached her breaking point. Parker had always loved the house I grew up in in Harlem and wanted nothing more than to move out of Brooklyn and fill up that four bedroom house with more babies. But we weren't exactly on the same page because I was perfectly content living in our cramped two bedroom apartment and never thinking of another kid after Nathan.

That's why I had been going so hard to sell the house because I knew if it wasn't in the family anymore then it would give me more time to convince her that we didn't need any more responsibilities. But I knew my days with her were numbered when Chris had decided to move there with Amber. It had already bothered her that Cam and Tillar were married and expecting a baby before us, but when the news broke that Chris of all people had settled down, it was like a slap in the face to her.

She had waited until before bed last Friday

night to tell me that she and Nathan were going to stay at her sister's place. I didn't question it because we had taken small breaks before, but the finality in her voice when she said they weren't coming back let me know this wasn't a drill anymore. But I knew it was for the best when I slept better than I had in a while that night.

We made sure to fuck every night since she had begun packing and that had to be a record for us because we had gotten down to just once a week in the previous year. It was almost back to feeling like it had in the beginning, but no matter how many times I made her legs tremble, she was intent on leaving today.

On Valentine's Day.

I had begged her to stay just one more night because of the snowstorm outside, but she said if she didn't do it while she was ready then she never would.

"Fine time to finally be sick of me," I joked to her about the weather as I looked at all of their boxes piled up around us. She finished taping up the last one on the floor before acknowledging my presence.

"I'm not sick of you, Chase. I'm leaving because I don't want to be sick of you," she said and even though I understood what she meant I thought it was a cop out because there was still no concrete reason for us to be breaking up. I could definitely see myself marrying her one day, but I didn't want to be pressured into it just because I wasn't on the same timeline as Cam and Chris.

Out of the corner of my eye I peeped Nathan's open doorway which exposed me to him packing up my PlayStation and Xbox. I had given them to him as a farewell since I had been putting off my real goodbye to him all week. I guess I was hoping that I wouldn't have to really say it, but Parker had given me back the keys and even started the process of getting her name off of the lease so I knew there was no going back now.

"Ay pick up that long face, Nate. I already ordered another system and you know we can still play online with the headsets," I told him as I put my hand on his shoulder, but he shrugged it off.

"It won't be the same," he said sadly and I sighed, feeling bad that I couldn't even tell him otherwise.

"I won't lie and say that it will be, but you know if you ever need something I'm here, right?" I asked and he slowly nodded. "Before you go I'm gonna let you in on a little secret, okay? I don't even really like kids, but you're the coolest little dude I know and anytime you want your favorite breakfast, just ask your moms to bring you by the restaurant and I'll make it for you, alright?"

He nodded again before Parker yelled out for him to go make sure he had everything he wanted to take with him today because they wouldn't be getting the rest until next week in a moving van.

I had gone back to tending to the soup I was making for Gram when I felt Parker's long arms wrap around my waist. I would especially miss that, her sneaking up on me and making my back just as warm and toasty as the heat made the front of me feel. She was the tallest woman I had ever dated and I didn't think I would ever not want to feel those long, shapely legs wrapped around me.

"Can we get some of that to go?" she asked about the soup. "You know Payton's fridge is perpetually empty," she reminded me about her older sister who had never liked me anyway, but I decided not to take one final dig at her and instead pleaded my case one more time.

"You can have as much as you want if you tell me that this is only temporary and you're not giving up on us, P," I told her as I turned to face her. She sighed, but the frustration she obviously felt with me still wasn't evident in her voice.

"Chase, you gave up on us long before I ever did. And I just wish I knew the reason why," she said sounding eerily similar to Nathan. And even though her words grammatically made a statement, I knew she was still asking that same question that we had been fighting over for way too long.

Is there somebody else?

I felt even worse knowing that I could pinpoint the exact night that had led us here, but I would never tell her the truth. The old Chris would've been proud of me for not copping to cheating because there was no proof of it, but lying to her still hadn't kept her here with me so it was just another useless secret now.

But instead of letting her know that she had been right about everything all along, I just kissed her lips one last time and felt relieved when she kissed me back. The relief didn't last long though because her next words felt like she was putting the final nail in our relationship's coffin.

"Whoever she is, I hope you're better to her than you were to me," she said not really sounding like the *not jealous* but territorial Parker I had always known.

"I already told you that there is nobody else and even if it was, I know you don't really mean that."

"Actually I do because I also sincerely hope she puts you through the wringer," she said with a bittersweet smile before putting her lips on mine again. "Goodbye Chase Logan."

"See you at brunch with Gram on Sunday, Parker Reynolds," I said trying to see if she would go for it.

"Oh please. We are not in a relationship anymore so I no longer have to kiss your grandma's evil ass," she laughed out, but it was fucked up because we had been such good friends before and we both knew that we probably wouldn't be anymore. At the very least I was happy that we were ending things civilly though.

"My Gram's not evil. She just doesn't like you," I finally admitted because I had been denying the obvious truth for the entirety of our relationship.

"I knew it!" she exclaimed along with a slap on my arm which caused me to laugh too.

Gram had never been nasty to her or anybody else that she wasn't fond of, but she just had a certain way of talking to the people she did like that it was always easy to tell where you stood with her.

By the time I had finished packing up the soup in a big Tupperware bowl, they were gone and I was officially alone on Valentine's Day. I wasn't really much of a sentimental dude, but it did hit me that this was probably the first time I'd never had a Valentine. When I called my Gram and told her that, she smiled and said that just like when I was a boy she would be my Valentine then asked me to stay with her for the night since I would be bringing her soup soon anyway.

We were supposed to be going to Atlanta for

Cam and Tillar's baby shower tomorrow, but she'd been sick all week so we had canceled the flights yesterday. And of course I felt bad that she wasn't feeling good, but I was relieved that I wouldn't be expected to go to the shower now and not just because I didn't want to see Cam.

It was because of Nicole.

She was Tillar's best friend so obviously she would be there, but I still wasn't ready to see her childish ass again yet. I probably should have been over the way she'd treated me by now, but it had been almost a year and a half and our first and last phone conversation still left a bitter taste in my mouth.

"How could you change your mind already? You just said you couldn't wait to see me again too."

"Because that's what everybody says after a good nut, Chase, but nobody actually means that shit."

"Well I meant it. I was getting ready to break up with my girl for you and everything, Nicole."

"But who asked you to do that? Look you need to be thanking me because if new pussy has you ready to tap out and never go home again then you were wasting her time anyway."

"That's really how you feel?"

"I didn't stutter, did I?"

"Okay. Heard."

What really pissed me off though was that I

didn't even want to go to Cam's little make believe ball in the first place, but Gram wanted to so I had sucked it up and went. But little did I know that I would find not a princess of my own but a fucking magician there. I had been fresh off an argument with Parker and mad I had to be there at all so I was honestly just looking to fuck some rando before coming home, but before I knew it Nicole's little ass had put a spell on me.

I thought I knew what to expect when she, in her fitted Chun-Li costume, had invited me into her hotel room, but when she slowly undressed then let down her never-ending hair, I knew I was getting to meet Nicole for the first time and that shit was an introduction to remember. She was soft but dominant at the same time if that made sense and I had never been with a woman like that before.

"You will just lie here, okay? If you touch me I'm getting up and leaving."

I thought it was strange at the time, but I'd never had bad pussy from a crazy woman so I accepted her rules. It was tough, but I had just stuffed my hands behind my head and watched her go to work. It was all over her face that she enjoyed the ride and I remembered thinking that she may have hated men, but she sure as hell still loved dick.

Round two was much more intimate

though and even though she didn't say it, I could tell she didn't want to be alone that night because she began kissing me like a long-time lover and touching me like she knew my body. In the blink of an eye we were doing the closest thing to making love that two strangers could do, but I guess that shit meant more to me than it did to her because I was the one left wanting more than she was willing to give.

And I shouldn't have even been shocked by her cold demeanor afterwards because her reputation had preceded her. Most people on the internet just knew her as Cosplay Bae, but long before that she had fucked with a bunch of my frat brothers from Morehouse and even let some run a train on her so I also knew her as FreakNic. Trains were never my thing though because it always seemed suspect to be rock hard in a room full of other men, but to each his own.

And usually I didn't like going in after niggas I knew, but after hearing how good it was I wanted to have a FreakNic story of my own for the next Omega national leadership conference. But instead I had just been left with memories of holding her while she slept and her asking me to come back for an encore performance after we had to stay in town because of the fire at Cam's shop.

I didn't like to allow myself to think about

those nights too often because my body would react like she was really in front of me, but I couldn't stop myself from dreaming about it constantly. I would feel like shit for waking up with Nicole's name written on my erection and then using it on Parker, but I knew I would never get to use it on her again so I settled on the next best thing.

Thinking back on it all, I was dumb for even attempting to cuff her after only two nights especially because she wasn't the wifing type anyway, but I guess I just figured that we would have to find a way to make that shit work because I had never connected with somebody that much let alone so fast.

☗

On my way out the door with the soup for Gram my phone had vibrated in my pocket. I'd planned on ignoring it until I got to the car and thought that it could've been Parker calling to say she had changed her mind about everything. But to my surprise it was the last person I ever expected it to be and my heart nearly fell out of my chest when I saw Nicole's name on my home screen. I literally had to rub my eyes to make sure that I wasn't dreaming again because I had just fallen into a daydream and salivated at the thought of tasting her again.

I read over her message a few times a little confused because even though I couldn't hear her saying the words, it sounded like she was scared and that was not an emotion I had ever seen from her before. It just said that she was in my city and needed help so I temporarily put Gram's soup to the side because help was what I was gonna give her.

I knew the whole thing was nuts, but I guess I had just wanted to be the hero for at least one woman today. So far though I was just turning out to be an adversary to Nicole because after meeting up with her and dropping off Gram's soup, we'd had a little disagreement in my restaurant and we hadn't said a word to each other since.

I had been driving with an old school radio station turned down low for almost two hours, but not even the sweet sounds of Jeffrey Osbourne could cut through the tension in the car. And when she did finally decide to speak to me again it was only to let me know that she had to use the bathroom.

"And why are you telling me this?" I asked making myself keep my eyes on the road in front of me and not her because even though we were on the interstate the roads were still heavy with snow since there was hardly anybody crazy enough to be out in this weather.

"Hm maybe because I need you to find somewhere to stop so I can go."

"Look around you. Nothing's open and I can barely see the road signs as it is so I'm not going off course. You either gotta pop a squat in the pullover lane or hold it."

"Chase, I'm not peeing on the damn highway so go find somewhere that's not closed," she demanded like that was even possible.

"Okay and while I'm at it let me just snap my fingers and make a million dollars appear for you too," I said sarcastically before she kissed her teeth.

"You better do something unless you want me to piss on your seat," she said and from my peripheral I saw her cross her legs so I sighed then got off on the next exit.

I'd left my glasses in the restaurant so I had to squint to see the sign that told me we were in Scranton, Pennsylvania. I still didn't understand this weird ass interstate that took me through another state to get to Upstate New York, but I didn't plan on figuring it out tonight. I just wanted to get her there as fast as possible so she could go back to pretending like I didn't exist again.

I pulled up to a twenty-four hour gas station that was apparently closed for the storm, but I parked alongside a patch of thick bushes so that she could have some privacy. I shut off the engine and waited for her to get out, but she just looked over at me expectantly.

"I thought you had to go so bad."

"I do. Aren't you gonna get out with me?"

"For what? I don't have to pee."

"Well what if some creepy nigga or little rural critter attacks me?"

"Better you than me, Sister Souljah," I said just to be a dick to her since cooking for her and trying to be nice hadn't worked either. "And Scranton isn't rural. It just looks dead and deserted because of the storm."

"I don't care. Look can you just hold my hair up please? And don't try to look at me," she said before handing the unraveled ends of her braid to me and squatting outside on her side of the car.

For what it was worth I didn't look, but I had to say something after she had been out there and letting in all of that cold air for a couple minutes because it was beyond brick.

"Yo you got a bladder infection or something. Who pees this long?" I asked with more frustration than I actually felt because I didn't care about making the stop, holding her hair or even the cold. I cared that she was mad at me.

"Well it's cold as hell out here and I was

nervous on the plane so I had a lot to drink. Shit! My literal ass is about to freeze out here," she said chuckling at the predicament that she had found herself in. I wanted to laugh with her, but I didn't and just waited for her to get back in.

She let out a big breath of relief after closing the door and putting her seatbelt back on, but she groaned when she realized her phone, that she had been on nonstop while she ignored me, was about to die.

"Where's your charger?" she asked and I pointed to the glove department as I tried to find my way back around to the interstate. "Chase, this is for Androids. I have an iPhone."

"Oh then I guess you're shit out of luck then," I told her unsympathetically because now she would have to find something else to do with her time.

"Can I see your phone then?" she asked suddenly sounding like a nice little kid. I rolled my eyes before reaching in my pocket for it, but I didn't feel it on me.

"Fuck. I must've left it at the restaurant."

"You're joking, right?" she asked immediately switching back to bitch mode.

"What? I'll get it tomorrow. It was an honest mistake."

"Yeah and it could have been avoided if you were more worried about your phone than your fucking *Pokémon* bowls," she growled at me as she angrily crossed her arms over her chest.

"It's called a poke bowl and excuse me for not being obsessed with my phone and social media like some people."

"This has nothing to do with social media. What kind of person doesn't remember to grab their phone in this day and age? And in the middle of a storm at that?!"

"The kind of person who should have ignored the DM when they realized it was you," I said not even caring if we started arguing again because she was asking for it by being so mean and ungrateful.

"Please, you couldn't ignore me if you tried, *Chefboyardee*," she said and I nearly froze in my seat.

"What is that supposed to mean?"

"Stop playing in my face. I know that was you, Chase. And remind me never to commit a crime with you because you would for sure get us on the dumbest criminals list with your weak ass alias."

"I really don't know what you're talking about," I said trying to continue with the lie, but it was pointless because I really had dropped the ball with that name.

"Well do you know how much money you've spent getting your ass handed to you in 2K by me and the *real* goat Michael Jordan for the past year? Because I do," she said pulling my card about me wasting countless hours and money participating in this thing she did a few nights a week where she played videogames with her followers.

Of course I had made a fake page because I didn't want to embarrass myself any further, but because I didn't have a picture up she charged me since she only played for free with other women. I knew she must've been making bank doing that too because I was far from the only parched nigga who wanted her attention and most times I had to take a number.

"Okay so it was me. But it could've been anybody so aside from the name, how else did you know?" I asked curiously because we had never even spoken on the game.

"You always kept your mic muted. Literally every single nigga I play with wants to trash talk my ear off, but not Chefboyardee so it was obvious," she said and I had to applaud her investigative skills before finally getting back en route to Rochester.

"Yeah I didn't want you to recognize my voice."

"I know. That's why I even let you win sometimes for your trouble," she said sounding really southern for a minute, but I barely had time to think her accent was cute because I realized what she had said.

"Nah hold up. I won those games fair and square. I'm not even about to let you do that."

"Whatever helps you sleep at night, but trust me you men never know when women are faking it," she said before a long natural silence came over us for a few miles.

"Wait so if you knew that I was watching you all this time, does that mean that you were watching me too?"

"Only sometimes because you were really out here bad last year. Accidently liking then unliking my pictures, posting songs that were in my stories," she said before I decided to defend myself.

"You have good taste in music. So what?"

"I do. That's why Tillar always asks me to work with the DJs for her events. And everybody is still loving the playlist I made for the wedding," she said about to let the small compliment go to her head before suddenly turning to look at me. "Chase why weren't you at the wedding?" she asked curiously before I shrugged.

"I had other plans," I said curtly because I knew what she was getting at.

"More important than your brother's big day?"

"You sound like my Gram. Okay how about this? I'll try my best to make his next one. Happy now?" I asked sarcastically before she cut her eyes at me.

"Why the fuck would you say something like that? He's happy with Tillar," she informed me like I wasn't already aware, but I just shrugged again.

"He was happy with Summer too, but people change."

"Is that why you're so miserable now? You changed?"

"I'm far from miserable. I'm just finally starting to see this marriage shit for what it really is. Most relationships are meant to be temporary, but people are always forcing it and trying to stretch it out for a lifetime."

"So if you really feel like that then why were you so mad that I didn't let you break up with your girl for me? We would've just been temporary too, right?"

"Because there are exceptions to every rule and I was stupid enough to think that you could've been one."

"And what rule would that be Chase?"

"The one that says you should never try to turn a hoe into a housewife," I said looking over to see her reaction, but she was grinning like I had just told a joke.

"Well I guess you would know better than me because I've never tried to," she quipped.

"Don't worry. I learned my lesson."

"Aw knock it off. I did not break your heart."

"I never said you did. But my girl leaving and you being here today is showing me that I need to quit trying to be nice to women because you'll never appreciate it anyway. Single Chase is officially coming back."

"Single Chase? Is that like your even saltier alter ego?"

"Yeah, but his superpower is that he can sweet talk the panties off of the meanest woman in the world," I said smiling over at her to piss her off. "You see I tried using my powers for good, but y'all women only want men who are mean to you."

"Oh my God. Not you with this incel shit too," she said before rubbing her temples like I was irritating her.

"What? It's true. Think about it. We've been arguing since you got here, but I know for a fact that if you let me pull over and put my hand in your panties that you're probably dripping wet right now, aren't you?"

"Bruh, you have officially lost your rabbit ass mind. Any moisture currently in my panties is from having to drip dry after pissing outside. Not you."

"Let me feel then," I challenged her as I put my hand on her thigh, but she quickly moved it. "Scared?"

"No. Just not dumb enough to play these kinds of games. And if this is the way the conversation is headed then we can just go back to not talking at all," she said and I didn't fight it even though I'd wanted to keep the conversation going since arguing was better than nothing. But at least now I knew for sure that anything that involved me touching her pussy again was officially off the table.

We let the low radio and the sounds of the road take over for a while and without the aid of her phone she quickly found herself asleep with her head lulled against the foggy window. Without a watch or phone I didn't know how much time had passed because I barely diverted my eyes from the few cars in front of me, but at least another two hours had to have gone by since we were getting close to Syracuse.

Michael Jackson was singing about butterflies when she sat up to stretch and yawn. I let a few minutes go by before speaking again because I didn't want it to seem like I had missed hearing her voice or anything like that.

"So are we ever gonna talk about this weird hair flex thing you're doing? I saw on one of your

Question and Answer videos that you've never had a haircut in your life, just trims. What, are you scared you're a descendent of Samson?" I asked already going back on my word and trying to be nice to her again.

"No. It's because before I was FreakNic, I was Rapunzel. She was the only princess I could identify with because in the original fairytale she was given away at birth," she said and I believed her until she cracked a smile. "You are so gullible. I just like having long hair. I grew up Jehovah's witness and I liked pissing off the elder members who used to tell Winnie to cut it."

"Winnie? That's your adopted mother's name?"

"No 'adopted'. Winnie was just my mama. Her and Henry weren't perfect, but they were too good to me to not give them the respect of those titles."

"If they were so good to you then why are you on this grail quest to find the people who gave you up?"

"Because I have a right to know who they are. Why are you worried about it in the first place?"

"I'm really not. What are you doing?" I asked as she took off her seatbelt all of a sudden.

"Getting a sandwich. I'm hungry."

"Get me one too," I told her before she moved closer to me to reach the cooler in the backseat.

With a good amount of her hair in my face I got a nose full of the scent of fresh picked berries coming from it. I was in a daze for a second thinking back on those two nights when she had let it cover our bare bodies like her strands made up the finest afro textured bedsheets money could buy before I refocused and shook it off.

I reached over for one of the prosciutto and Swiss sandwiches in her hand, but she refused to give it to me.

"Are you planning on getting off at the exit to eat? Because I'm not letting you drive with one hand," she said sounding like I was a passenger in her car and not the other way around.

"Whatever just put some of it in my mouth then," I said frustrated before realizing how it came off. "Ay that's what she said," I laughed out trying to have a goofy moment with her, but her face remained still.

"You know at first I thought it was Chris, but you're the real final boss of fuckboys, aren't you?" she said as she unwrapped her sandwich then took a big bite and almost moaned when it hit her taste buds. "Damn. Now this is really good. I can't believe you're missing out on this. And that little bit of homemade mayo and Dijon mustard is really working well here. My compliments to the chef," she said sarcastically before going in for more.

I just rolled my eyes then carefully switched lanes to get off at the next exit because my stomach was beginning to growl and I did finally have to pee. Plus after being on the road for over four hours straight I needed a break anyway because I was used to being in bed at this time of night. I drove around the snow covered area for a couple minutes looking for a place to park when I saw a sign for a drive-in not too far away then laughed to myself.

"What's so funny?"

"Nothing. Just that my dad took my mother on their first date in this car and it was to a drive-in just like this out in Queens."

"Well this is far from a date so I'm not seeing the irony," she said with her mouth full and I just sighed because I wasn't trying to imply that this situation was romantic at all.

"Why can't you ever just fucking relax? For your next costume I think you should try cosplaying as a sane person because it's not adding up. You claim you hate men so much, but you surround yourself with us and still fuck us. The math ain't mathin'."

"Do the science then," she said with a shrug.

"Okay so just answer me this then. If you

really hate niggas like you say you do then why don't you just go eat some pussy and leave us alone?"

"Believe me I've tried, but unfortunately I just can't," she said with a sigh as I smirked and licked my lips.

"Wait, you really tried?"

"Yeah and I can attest to the fact that religious folks got it all wrong. If being gay was a choice I would be laid up with a woman who looks just like me right now."

"You're really that pleased with yourself, huh?" I asked clearly amused that she would fuck herself.

"I paid enough to be," she said shamelessly referring to getting plastic surgery.

"So how can you even claim to be a feminist then when you chopped and screwed your body just to look good for men?"

"Because I recognize reality and looking a certain way equals better treatment. There's a sucker like you born every day who'll pay cold hard cash just to *virtually* be in the presence of a woman who looks like me," she said confidently, but I just scoffed and didn't say anything because I knew my bank statements proved her point. "And do you really think Cam would be taking care of Tillar like he does if she looked like Shrek? No. Men can walk around looking like a germ, but there's power in beauty for us. I recognize that this world is fucked, but that doesn't mean I can't benefit from it when and if I choose to because y'all do it all the time," she said before finally giving me the sandwich, but I told her to hold it while I leaned over to pee out of the slightly open door. The snow was deep as hell so there was no way I was stepping one foot outside.

"Be careful with that. We wouldn't want your brain getting caught in your zipper," she quipped.

"Yeah yeah. You just try not to look either."

"Not like there's much to see anyway," she said trying to be funny, but I didn't even bother responding because I remembered that startled look on her face when she first slid down on me and by the end she didn't know if she was coming or going.

We sat not really saying much to each other but instead just enjoyed the food and the calm of the quiet while big snowflakes continued adding to the ample supply all around us. I noticed that the gas was getting low, but I estimated that we were about an hour and a half away and the amount left should've just gotten us there.

"You look exhausted. Want me to take it from here?" she offered when I was getting ready to head back over to the interstate.

"That depends on if you can actually see over the steering wheel," I cracked on her lack of height.

"I think I can handle it and you can finally get some sleep," she said sounding like she was really appreciative of me for the first time all night.

Neither one of us wanted to get out and walk around in all those feet of snow so we Tetris'd our way around until I was in her seat and she was in mine. For a brief couple seconds she was seated on my lap, but she quickly maneuvered so that it was over just as it had really began.

It didn't hit me until she was backing out that I hadn't been a passenger in the Bluebird since before my dad died and it was the last gift he'd given me before passing. Out of the three of us I was always the one down to help him work on her even into adulthood so it was a no brainer when he asked what belongings of his I wanted for myself.

And of course losing my old man was devastating and I still didn't feel completely over it, but hitting the streets in his car did always make me feel like he was still along for the ride with me. I closed my eyes and thought about all of the good times we had in here, but before Nicole could even get out of the parking area she had ran something over and I'd hit my head on the roof of the car on impact.

"Fuck! Are you alright?" she asked clearly shaken up by the bump too.

"What the fuck was that?" I asked rubbing the top of my head because that shit had really just hurt a lot.

"I don't know. Let's see," she said like we were about to go on a scavenger hunt or something.

I grumbled to myself as the cold snow hit halfway up my jeans while I struggled to walk around and see what she had hit. There was no blood so I knew it wasn't an animal, but I could see something black stuck in the front tire on the driver's side. Upon inspection I saw that it was completely blown out and for a minute I felt like I was in *Jeepers Creepers* until I realized that she'd hit a knocked over grill that had been covered in the snow.

And even though it was obviously not done on purpose that didn't stop me from losing my cool and yelling at her about being so reckless and not watching where she was going.

"Look I said I'll pay for the damages, but you got me fucked up if you think you're gonna be talking to me any kind of way over some old ass car."

"It's not just some old ass car. And I've never had to get any extensive work done on it because I'm always careful, but one night, hell one minute with you behind the wheel and my shit is totaled," I said exaggerating.

"It's not totaled. It's just this front part right here. Just change the tire and we'll be out of here."

"I can't change it," I said more to myself as I looked around finally realizing what was going on. We had no access to a phone, a limited supply of gas, and the location of the drive-in was in a mostly secluded part of whatever Upstate town we were in.

"Why can't you change it?" she asked with an attitude before burping loudly.

"Well that's not very ladylike," I said sarcastically as I stood to my feet and realized that it looked like she was standing in quicksand compared to me because the snow was almost at her waist.

"Does it look like I care? Just wait until that asparagus you fed me earlier makes its way down and I have to fart. Then I'll really show you how ladylike I am. But you know what is ladylike? Not knowing how to change a damn tire," she said as she dragged her legs back over to the driver's seat before she got too cold.

I told her to quickly pop the trunk for me then I got out the few picnic blankets that I kept in there for the rare occasions that Parker, Nathan and I could make it to Central Park. They were the only thing in there that would prove helpful to me now since I had left my jack in her car the last time I changed her tire.

"And just for the record I know how to change a tire just not in fifty fucking feet of snow without a jack," I told her as I got back inside and kicked off as much snow as I could. I gave her two of the blankets for her legs and kept one for myself.

"Can't you just lift it?" she asked and I could tell she actually thought that was possible.

"Can't you just lift it?" I asked mocking her. "No I'm not *Strong Guy* so I can't lift a heavy ass car."

"Oh so I guess those fake ass muscles really are just for show, huh?"

"I know you're not calling shit on me fake when I'm willing to bet that your hair is the only thing real on you," I said matter-of-factly because even in her loose fitting clothes I could still see that her breasts were slightly too big for her small frame. I couldn't tell if she'd had work done on her butt though because her thighs were proportionate and it moved and felt real.

"And yet you still can't keep your eyes to yourself," she said smugly.

"Yeah well it's only because I'm wondering if those ass shots leaked and travelled up to your brain yet."

"No ass shots over here, sweetheart. Try again."

"Oh so you were fat like Tillar and got lipo and a Brazilian Butt Lift, huh?"

"Ooh you sure do know a lot about women's medical procedures, *sus*. Why didn't you use all of this knowledge to get a BBL for your girl Pancake Parker?" she said cockily because the night we first fucked I had told her how I thought her body was perfect since it looked just like the women from comics that I grew up fantasizing about.

"Ay don't ever say her fucking name. You don't know shit about her!" I barked at her more out of guilt than anything.

"You need to lower your fucking tone before I tell her how you let me ride your face then sent you back home to kiss her. *I ain't a spiller, but don't push me*," she warned me in a way that made me believe she would actually do it.

"And let's not even pretend for one fucking second that you wouldn't still devour my *fake ass* again right now if I offered you another lick. Just look at how your immature ass practically nutted in your pants at the chance to be with me tonight," she said and I couldn't believe that she was questioning my mental age.

"Wait I'm immature? How about you're over thirty and still running around in costumes and playing videogames for a living? You dress like you're SuperBitch every day but have the nerve to tell me I'm immature? You're really just like those confused ass feminists that I see in the restaurant every day," I said laughing at her because the audacity coming from her direction was astounding.

"No, actually I'm the rare breed of feminist that knows the only way to true female liberation is to kill all of y'all and burn this shit to the ground. I just gotta convince other women to get on board first," she said in all seriousness.

"Yo you think you're so fucking real and down for the female cause, don't you? But you're not Susan B. Anthony. You're a clown with Wi-Fi. A City Girl with a wack ass Women's Studies degree. You're a bad influence on women, making them look over their shoulder and scared of all men. I should have known Chris's wife was one of your minions when I met her because she acts just like you."

"Not possible. She's married with a baby so she must've been faking it until she made it."

"No, she's the real deal. She's walking around with his balls in her Chanel purses now."

"Maybe for a little while but not forever. I've only met him once, but even I instantly knew he wasn't wrapped too tight either."

"Trust me, you would love him now since he's been neutered," I assured her, but she just shook her head. "So according to you there's no way to be with a man and still believe what you do?"

"In theory it is but not in practice."

"So you're just gonna be alone forever?"

"I'm not alone. I have a best friend, two businesses, hobbies and dick on demand. What else do I need?"

"Somebody who you don't have to put up a front for," I said simply.

"And I guess that was supposed to be you, huh? You're already whining about a fucking burp, but you expect me to believe that you would've accepted all of me?" she asked rhetorically, but I didn't plan on answering anyway because she had a point. "For whatever reason you seem to think you're so different from other bum ass niggas, but you're just like them. Admit it. You only wanted a fantasy out of me too and you forgot that Nicole Chante Jones is a real person underneath these costumes and FreakNic tales."

"Did I forget or did you forget? Because I'm not the one pretending like being alone and turning their life into an episode of *Sex and the City* is the answer to everything."

"I didn't say it was the answer to everything, but it's definitely the answer to not ending up with a walking, *cheating* headache like you," she said really putting the emphasis on *cheating* to fuck with me.

"You know you actually are kind of like Rapunzel except instead of letting down your hair you just let down your panties for everybody, right?" I said trying to hit her where it would hurt, but she was playing good defense just like she always did in 2K.

"And you're kind of like a Chad or a Jason except your parents were too dumb to pick one."

"Did your parents even bother naming you at all before they left you at the fire station?" I asked and immediately felt like I had gone too far, but she didn't react to it so I wouldn't bother saying sorry even though I wished I could take that one back.

"Fuck you. And if I die here, I swear to God I'm haunting your tall Whitebeard looking ass forever," she said comparing me to this big ass anime character and I almost laughed, but the thought of being stuck out here long enough to die kept me angry enough to fire back.

"No if I die here then God is gonna have to forgive me for going upside your head in the afterlife because I could've been at the crib sleeping right now."

"Please, this is the most exciting thing that's happened to you since you met me," she said sounding full of herself, but I just ignored her and tried to focus on the few survival skills I knew of to get us back home in one piece because shit was starting to look grim.

3

TRAP OR DIE

NICOLE

So this was how I was gonna die, huh? Trapped in a freezing cold car with a man. I mean freezing to death would be bad enough on its own, but somehow throwing in the set of XY chromosomes that made up Chase Logan made everything worse and I didn't deserve this.

Yeah sure I wasn't exactly Mother Teresa, but I still thought that I would get a better ending to my story than this because I was only ever mean to men and I'd never seen a woman doing something amazing and not hyped her up for it. But none of that mattered because it had been hours since I blew out the tire and nobody had came along to help as the storm grew worse and the snow mounted up around us.

It was cold and I was shivering, but luckily Chase had blankets on standby and knew that he should start the car for ten minutes every hour to keep us relatively warm. We didn't have a clock so we had just been alternating keeping track of ten minutes at a time until we could turn it on again.

At one point he had even gotten out and wrote HELP in purple in the snow with the ingredients from the acai bowls in case a plane was flying over. It was quickly covered up by more snow, but I remembered thinking that even though he was annoying he was also resourceful as fuck.

During a set of his ten minutes I sat and thought about how I had ended up here. And even though I had left religion behind after Winnie and Henry died I still prayed to myself for a while and asked Jehovah to see us home.

And speaking of them, I had always felt bad for feeling like I could finally be myself or rather the person I had always wanted to be after they passed. But while being rewarding, being their daughter had also been restricting in so many ways so when they were gone I decided to do everything that I could never do when they were alive. I celebrated every holiday down to Groundhog Day and got fucked up every single birthday like it would be my last.

I even finally worked up the nerve to get my surgeries because I had always been teased for lacking curves. And after I'd started wearing less and going out more, the rest was history. So yeah I guess since all of that had led me right here to this very spot, that dying trying to find my real parents would be my karma. Because if I had just been content with the life they'd given me then I would've been home now anyway.

Chase's calm, but heavy breathing as he counted lowly to himself brought me back to the current state of things and it made me think about how everything had been going fine the first couple hours. We weren't talking because I had been giving him the silent treatment, but the music on the radio had been good and I'd had enough juice on my phone to keep me preoccupied.

Tillar had been asking for updates every step of the way then and concerned that I was texting her back so fast while I was supposed to be driving so I finally had to let her know the deal.

"Chase is driving. And please just don't even ask."

"I won't. Just use a condom."

I didn't even respond to her insinuation that we would have sex again and instead just let her know that I was beating her ass as soon as she had that baby.

I sighed hard when Chase looked over and announced that it was my turn to count again because I was over the whole thing. If I died, I died.

"Okay can we just stop all of this fucking

counting and survivalist shit you're doing because it's driving me nuts?"

"How else do you think we'll be able to tell how much time has passed? We don't exactly have a lot of gas left to be guessing."

"Well figure something else out because hopefully it won't be long until somebody finds us. This is a big as public parking lot so I'm sure the owner will have somebody coming to plow and put down salt soon," I told him thinking on the spot because as a southern girl I didn't really know anything about this stuff.

"I'm surprised you would even trust a plow man to rescue you since his job is to be outside in the dark."

"What is that supposed to mean?"

"I watched your video on how you think men should have curfews when the sun goes down," he said and I groaned at him bringing up yet another topic for us to fuss about, but I guess I didn't mind it as much now because at least his hot breath was helping to keep the car warm.

"And? I've done my research and a curfew for y'all would immediately cut the rates for most violent crimes in half and damn near eliminate the chance for others."

"That's impossible and literally the stupidest thing I've ever heard in my life."

"How? Y'all clearly don't know how to act

any time of the day, but the freaks really do come out at night."

"But that won't solve everything because a man intent on hurting somebody would just do it when he is allowed out."

"My point exactly. That's why the curfew is just phase one. Phase two is eventually limiting the number of males born, but I haven't uploaded that video yet," I told him matter-of-factly.

The only reason I hadn't was because I wasn't prepared for the backlash I would get from my newest subscribers just yet. Dealing with men in person was already a tossup of Jekyll or Hyde, but dealing with them online was guaranteeing yourself that you would see their dark side.

People, but especially men always thought I was being dramatic about this shit until I started showing the amount of death and rape threats and doxxing attempts I got daily just for daring to have a platform and calling myself a feminist.

"Please tell me you're joking, right?" he asked, but I wasn't. "Well what about your male family members? You said your dad was good to you so would you be okay with him suffering because of what other men did?" he said trying to pull on my heartstrings, but it didn't work.

"He was good to me because I was his daughter, but even I don't know how he treated women before he got with Winnie. Every man has a mother and many have daughters, but that doesn't stop them from actively participating in the worst forms of misogyny. And being a good dad doesn't mean you're a good man," I said and it made me think about how Cam had once said his dad was both because he didn't play about his integrity.

"You bring up my daddy while failing to realize that he's the one who taught me not to trust y'all. And as for other quote unquote *good men* who haven't done one single thing to dismantle patriarchy, fuck them too because silence is complicity and they know they benefit from it. You men are always talking about *protecting and providing* without ever acknowledging who the fuck we need protecting from! Well guess what? It's y'all! You know how many women will be killed by a man she laid next to at some point? Way more than those that are killed by strangers and it's even higher for black women so no I'm not joking about a theory that would protect women who look like me!" I shouted at him then found myself almost out of breath from the mouthful I had just thrown his way.

"Alright alright. Calm down. You made your point."

"Don't tell me to calm down. If this same conversation was about white people or even just white men you wouldn't bat an eyelash because they're the ones with their foot on your black ass neck!"

"Nobody has their foot on my neck."

"Yes the fuck they do. You can't fool me. Every time a cop pulls you over, I bet you're shaking in your big ass strolling boots like a little bitch."

"That's completely different and you know it."

"Is it? Because I have the same feeling with cops that I have with y'all and that should bother you, but I know it doesn't."

"It does bother me. And that's why I go out of my way to make women feel safe around me."

"You want a cookie for that, Ted Bundy? Because it's a known fact that women should never trust a man trying to look like he's trustworthy."

"Well it must be working because you called me when you were in a bind."

"Only because there was nobody else to call."

"Tell yourself whatever you want, but a woman like you always has options, Nicole," he said and I could tell that he meant it in a few different ways. "So be real with yourself about why you made me your first one."

By that point I was so worked up and angry

that I just started counting again because I had to get my mind off of this situation and how cold my fingers kept getting every time he turned off the gas and heat.

I guess me blowing on them must've been irritating him because he suddenly took off his gloves then handed them over to me.

"Thank you," I said as I put them on then looked up expecting him to do the same with his hat because my head was cold too.

"No. You better wrap your hair up in a turban or something. Cold hands I can deal with but not a cold head."

"Okay I have an idea then. Let's get in the backseat."

"What for?" he asked suspiciously because it would put us further away from the main source of heat.

"Because I like having toes more than I dislike you. We need to huddle up instead of trying to keep warm separately and build more layers with these blankets."

I watched him slowly climb back there before I followed his lead and sat next to him. As he straightened out the blankets I began unraveling my hair so that I could let it down and use it strategically.

"What are you doing?" he asked me with confused brows as I began wrapping it around him a few times.

"I'm making you a headscarf so that I can have your hat. See you're not the only one who can survive in the wild," I said lightheartedly to him while I made a hole for his face to peek out of.

"Mm that feels good. Thank you," he said before turning to me. "This is cool for now, but I think we would do better if we were facing each other and you put your arms inside my coat sleeves," he suggested before I frowned at him.

"Did you learn that in the Boy Scouts?" I teased him before he kissed his teeth.

"No. It's just common sense because of our body heat. Let's try it," he said before lifting then putting me in the position he wanted which was basically me straddling him.

I went along with it though because even though his hands were cold, he was right about his chest still being warm. We were awkwardly face to face because of how I was sitting and my hair being wrapped around him so I just laid my head on his shoulder and began counting down until we could turn the gas back on.

Our cores were pressed together and his arms were wrapped around me for approximately one ten minute session before I felt it moving underneath me.

"Chase, what could possibly be appealing about the situation we're in right now? Why is your damn dick getting hard?" I asked almost surprised that he couldn't control himself even at a time like this.

"Well for one, you're sitting right on it and keeping it warm," he reasoned so I moved to sit more on his thigh, but he quickly put me back on it. "No. If there's one part of me that I don't want to get frostbitten, it's that so you just gotta chill out for me."

"I don't think so. You better use your hands, not the fat from the fake ass you were just talking shit about," I said smugly.

"Alright. I'm sorry. If it's any consolation it feels real, alright? Hats off to your surgeon," he said desperately and I just shook my head to avoid laughing at how big of a fool he was.

It was actually one of the things that had attracted me to him since funny men used to be my weakness and it certainly didn't hurt that he was nice to look at too, but I would never tell him that.

I did my best to ignore what was happening underneath me and before we knew it, it was time to turn the gas back on. But after he reached past me to do it, I realized that he wasn't holding onto me like a person desperate to get warm anymore. He was holding me like he knew he would never get to do it again and that made me pull back to see his face.

"Oh please don't tell me you're some undercover hopeless romantic like Cam because I didn't get that vibe from you at all."

"What?" he asked playing dumb.

"You still like me, don't you, Chase?"

"No. What would make you think that?"

"Um…maybe the fact that you've anonymously spent thousands of dollars on me, you obviously watch all of my YouTube videos on both channels, and last but not least you're stuck out here with me when you had plenty of opportunities to say no. I think one of those things but especially all three point to the math ain't mathin'," I said mocking what he'd said earlier.

"So do the science then," he said smiling. "I mean obviously I don't hate you or else I wouldn't be here, but I wouldn't say I like you either because you're a walking pain in the ass," he told me while we were almost nose to nose and breathing on each other.

"I find that hard to believe. If I was the relationship type you would definitely be all over me."

"Nah. I'm not Chris. After working hard all day all I want is for somebody to rub my back then ride my face not bring up everything that's wrong with men all the time," he said with a smirk like he knew I would do that, but I just shrugged.

"Why not get a girl that could do both? That way you get the best of both worlds," I said sarcastically, but he waved off the idea of dating a feminist woman.

"Enough about me. I'll be fine. But what are we gonna do about you because the idea of being single forever doesn't sound fun?"

"Not always but neither is being with somebody all the time."

"It is with the right somebody."

"You really believe that?"

"Sometimes," he said after pensively thinking it over for a minute and something about those few lines that had formed on his forehead and the way his body felt beneath me made me want to put my lips on his so I did it. "Whoa what was that for?"

"Because I know you've been wanting to do it all night and it's the only way that I can thank you if we don't make it out of this," I said before going in for another one and finally feeling scared enough about not surviving to tell him how I really felt.

"Chase, you weren't wrong about the whole spark thing before. I did feel it too. But ultimately I know that being with a man and feeling stuff like that is just not for me. Hell Tillar thinks I'm crazy because I won't even find somebody to marry just so I can get my inheritance in full," I joked, but he just looked at me sideways.

"Wait what?"

"Yeah before Henry died, he drew up a whole new will that said I would only get a monthly stipend instead of all the money at once unless I was married."

"But why would he do that when he told you not to trust men?"

"That's precisely why he did it. Just like he knew I would never get married, he also knew how bad I was with money back then and I would have probably blown through it all had he not set it up that way. But I'm sure the biggest reason was so that I wouldn't ever have to depend on a man for anything because my next big paycheck would always only be a month away for the rest of my life."

"That's actually really smart, but I'm glad my dad didn't pull that shit or else I would've been married just long enough to deposit the check," he said causing us both to laugh, but he suddenly stopped before I did. "I'll tell you what, Miss Nicole Chante Jones. If we do make it out of this alive, then I'll marry you, but you gotta let me be the one to file the divorce papers," he said with a sneaky look on his face.

"I'm desperate, Chase, but not that

desperate," I said with a grin until I saw that he wasn't smiling. "You're serious?"

"Yeah it wouldn't be real and it'll be just until you get your money."

"Well how much do you want then because I'm not giving more than ten percent?" I said definitively because I had already crunched the numbers before. Now he was smiling.

"You don't have to pay me for this."

"I don't understand. Why would you do it then?"

"Because of the spark," he said before letting his lips brush against mine again. "And so I can be the only man to get you to settle down. Plenty of niggas have had FreakNic, but I want to be the only man to say he got Nicole even if it's just for a little while," he said then paused like he was expecting a response, but I couldn't give him anything. "Did I say something wrong?"

"No. I don't know Maybe," I said trailing off into my own thoughts, but he wouldn't let me stay there.

"What is it?" he asked sounding a little concerned which made me sigh because I really didn't feel like reliving shit that I purposely kept buried inside.

"Nothing. I don't talk about my woes with men. My daddy taught me that y'all are all just like white folks, always wanting our rhythm but not our blues," I told him then hated that it was so cold because I felt my eyes getting watery thinking about Henry, the only man I would ever love.

"Well I've already had the rhythm so I guess you've earned the right to give me some of your blues too," he said with his lips still against mine. "Tell me what's on your mind. No judgement," he promised, but it still took a while for me to work up the nerve to say the words.

"Chase, a long time ago I said I would never let myself be alone with another Que like you," I told him simply as I touched the branding on his arm hoping that he read between the lines so I wouldn't have to say it.

"Why, because fraternities represent patriarchy for you or something?"

"No because I don't trust men as individuals let alone men who run in packs, but I had the misfortune of befriending a few Ques back when I was still pretending that *not all men* were capable of being bad."

"And what are you saying?" he asked as he shifted a little underneath me.

"I'm saying that whatever you may have heard about me from those niggas in your frat is true. I had sex with almost the whole spring line back when I was a freshman at Spelman," I told him honestly and the car was suddenly so quiet that the gulp from him swallowing his spit could've caused an echo.

"But let them tell it I just up and decided to have sex with all of them in the same night, right? Not that I was there to get my Biology notes back from Alex and the rest of them trapped me in his room?"

"Wait? Y-You mean they hurt you?" he stammered out and I could practically see the flames building behind his eyes.

"Yes and no. I've seen enough *Law & Order* to know what was about to happen to me and I didn't want to be a victim so I told them they didn't have to hold me down or force me. I just did it willingly and," I began but continued watching his face because he was stone cold quiet.

"It was weird because it was the first time that I realized that I could actually control men. I made them use condoms and go one at a time. And yeah I was tired and sore when I got back to my dorm and people started talking shit about me afterwards, but I justified it because in my mind at least I wasn't *really* raped. And for years after that I convinced myself that I would much rather be called a hoe than hurt any day, but these days I'm not so sure. So now you know the truth. That's the *real* story of how FreakNic came to be."

Chase was quiet with his eyes closed for what felt like hours but was actually just a minute or two before expelling all the breath in his body. It felt good on my face though so I had no complaints as I waited to see if I was wrong about telling him something that I had never told a soul before. Not even Tillar.

"You did what you had to do to make it home, Nicole. And I'm so fucking sorry for calling you that. I promise it'll never happen again," he said as he squeezed me tighter and cradled my head to his chest.

"It's okay. You didn't know," I said trying to minimize how much hearing him call me that throughout the night had actually hurt my feelings.

"I shouldn't have had to know. I know better than to disrespect a woman no matter how mad I get. And I just want you to know that if I ever get home again, I'm quitting my organization. I don't want any association with them anymore," he said definitively which made me raise my head to look at him.

"But why? You think that's the first time dudes in your frat did something like that to a girl?"

"I'm not that naïve, Nicole, but it's the first time that it's brothers I know. And it's you so that makes all the difference in the world to me."

I didn't know what to say because I had never heard a man speak that way about me before. I had honestly expected him to react differently because men didn't exactly respond to rape sympathetically most of the time.

"Any excuse not to pay your membership dues anymore, huh?" I said trying to clear out some of the heaviness. It worked because I heard the smile in his voice and shivered when he moved some hair out of the way to kiss the top of my head.

"That's not it. I just know what I would do if I was ever in the same room with any of them again so I'm taking preventative measures because I can't protect you from prison."

"I don't need protecting, Chase. And I don't want or need some Prince Charming like other women," I told him proudly because this occasion was the first in years that I'd been anywhere without my gun.

"Then I guess that just means I'll have to be your knight in shining armor, huh?" he suggested instead.

"Same difference. A rose by any other name," I began but he finished the classic line from Shakespeare for me.

"Would smell as sweet. You're not the only one who paid attention in high school English class, Nicole," he joked before tightening his grip on me. "And you're right. It doesn't matter what we call what I am to you because I already know what you've been to me since that first night."

"And what's that?" I asked then found myself anxiously waiting for the answer that sat on the tip of his tongue much too long for my liking.

"You're the one that got away," he nearly whispered into my mouth which suddenly caused a stirring in my core. He was giving me butterflies. "And I swear if it wasn't so cold I would take all of this shit off and show you just how bad I've been missing you all this time," he said with so much sincerity that it warmed my body all over.

"I don't want to die here, Chase," I told him feeling my eyes get heavy with tears.

"You're not going to. I'll make sure of that. But even if we do, I'm glad I got to at least make shit right with you before the end," he said as he looked into my eyes and it made me sigh.

"You don't even know me."

"I like what I know," he said before turning the gas off and starting to count again.

♕

Dawn had barely painted the night sky when I heard someone tapping on the window to Chase's car. I hurried and woke him up since we had somehow fallen asleep the last time that he'd started up the car so it was still relatively warm and toasty inside.

"You folks alright in there?" a loud man's voice asked and I had never been so happy to hear a baritone like his in my life.

It wasn't the plow man but just a run of the mill good Samaritan who gave us a ride to a nearby motel and who let me charge my phone so that we could get a mechanic to come out and get the car as soon as possible.

Chase's legs were weak and numb from the cold and me sitting on them for so long so we slowly made our way inside the building.

"One room or two?" the guy behind the front desk asked us and Chase looked at me to decide.

"Just one," I said as he handed over a credit card and tried to hide his smile.

After carefully getting him to the room, I laid him back and checked his feet because I had been worried about the way he was walking.

"Well the good news is they're not frostbitten. The bad news is they're still ugly as hell," I told him because I was obviously in a much better mood since I knew I wouldn't be kicking the bucket just yet.

His teeth chattered as he spoke, "If only your followers could see you now. Happily taking care of a man."

"It's only because I don't need you losing any body parts before I get to enjoy them one more time," I told him as I got in bed next to him.

"Just one more time?" he asked and it caught me off guard.

"For now," I told him honestly because I hadn't thought that far ahead yet.

He was still shivering pretty badly because he had done a much better job keeping me bundled up so I decided to do what I knew would help thaw him out a little faster. I put one of his cold hands between my thighs to quickly warm it up then put the other inside of my shirt.

Before long he was practically as good as new and back to being the old annoying Chase by exaggerating that the hair down south was getting just as long as the hair on my head. I had been freshly waxed last time I saw him and I almost explained that the baby shower had kept me too busy to get one, but I decided against it.

"Do you want it or not?" I challenged him as he ran his fingers through the soft hairs on my pussy before landing on my clit. I tried to keep a pokerface, but I was already flushed down there and on my face.

"I want it however you want to give it to me," he said sincerely and it sent a chill up my spine.

I reached over and grabbed onto him,

suddenly remembering the last time I'd held it in my hand. I thought it was a feat that he didn't lose consciousness with all the blood that it must have taken to keep that big thing erect.

When he entered me again I swear it was like no time had passed since the last time we'd done this. He gave me the same delicate kisses from before and stared as deeply into my eyes as he was deep inside of me. We had built up plenty of tension over the course of the night, but it still didn't feel like we were in a hurry to finish.

For me it was almost like an out of body experience and I felt like I was watching myself holding onto him for dear life as he stroked me so good. And I swear it didn't even feel like there was anything between us even though I had made sure there was this time.

"That's how you like it, huh?" he asked me softly when he felt my thighs and pussy twitching underneath him as he gave it all to me slowly.

"Yes Chef," I moaned in his ear and almost caused him to fall off of me.

"Fuck Nicole! Ay don't say that shit again until I'm ready to come, alright?" he groaned out and I laughed.

I was so happy that neither of us had lost the feeling in our fingers because we caressed each other and savored the moment like we knew we might never get to do it again. But I wouldn't lie anymore. This was something like I had never felt before even with him. And as much as I didn't want it to end, even more so I didn't want to only just do it this once because at the moment nothing in the world but what was underneath those sheets mattered.

As he gave me the last few powerful but calculated strokes to make sure he didn't hurt me, I clung to him and found myself on the brink of tears as my orgasm clouded my vision and stirred my soul. All I saw was the white snow outside and me kissing him in the car so for a minute I thought I had actually died back there until I felt him giving me all that he had left before his own release came crashing down.

For a while we laid there refusing to let go of each other. He confessed that he had an important business meeting to get back to, but he said he would never leave this bed again if I stayed in it with him. He kissed each of my fingers one by one before I eventually surrendered to my exhaustion and fell asleep.

When we woke up a few hours later we had just enough time to take a quick shower and get dressed again before getting a call back from the mechanic. He had replaced the tire and he was even nice enough to offer to bring the car to us. Feeling satisfied and rested, I offered to drive the last stretch to Rochester, but I didn't even protest when Chase told me no. I just finally checked my missed calls and text messages including the one from BJ telling me that his mama, our mama was okay and recovering from her surgery.

The roads were still bad but getting cleared so we made it there in no time. Chase pulled up to the address of the hospital that BJ had sent me and was ready to hop out, but I stopped him because I wasn't. He must have known because he quickly hugged me then asked how I was feeling.

"I'm scared and I'm mad because the answers were right here in my face the whole time and I missed them. You know how much money I've wasted on this shit over the years?"

"Not as much as I have on restaurants," he said to get my mind off of it, but it didn't work.

"I guess I just don't understand because they're still together and they had three other kids after me so like why give me up? Why wasn't I good enough to keep?" I asked at the same time a tear came tumbling from my eye. He sighed as he stroked my back.

"We don't always understand why parents do what they do, but I like to believe that a good amount of the time it's because they think it's what's best for us. Sometimes they're wrong and sometimes they're right, but you had a good life, right?" he asked rhetorically, but I nodded anyway. "So forgive them. It sounds like they were just scared kids and they knew they would've probably fucked you up," he said trying to look on the bright side.

"But look at me. I'm still fucked up. I only have one friend and I'm so scared of my own shadow that I only feel safe when I have a gun on me," I told him honestly as more tears fell down, but he kept wiping as they came.

"No you're not. You're the least fucked up person I know. And you're not wrong about the shit you talk about men. A lot of that stuff is just hard to hear for the average person. But even if we are the weaker sex and we make the world a worse place to live in, I just want you to know that there's at least one of us trying to be better for the people we care about."

"You really care about me, Chase?" I asked sniffling back the last of my waterworks and I hated how damn needy I sounded all of a sudden.

"Too much. More than I care about the woman I thought I would spend my life with. And that's not a diss to her because letting Parker leave yesterday was one of the hardest things I'll probably ever do. But it's just a testament to how much I care about you. You got me out here half frozen and I'm definitely gonna be sick when I get home, but I don't even care. Because all of this came from making sure you were good and had what you needed," he said and I sighed in frustration. "What?"

"Nothing. But I can already tell you're gonna be the type of nigga I'll have to shoot for refusing to divorce me, aren't you?" I asked and he laughed.

"I mean I do still kinda want you and this to be mine for real," he said as he let his hand find its way back to my pussy.

"I know. That's why I let you borrow her again for a little while, but I'll always be the sole owner."

"Then you need to put me on the lease or something. I'll gladly pay rent because I like you, Nicole. I really like you."

"Aw hopefully it'll go away soon," I said in all seriousness so he tickled me. "What? I like you too, okay? But being with a man long term is just too big of a gamble and these days the only person I'm betting on is myself."

"I understand. Jumping into another relationship right now is the last thing I need, but when I'm ready I'm gonna give you a call and see if you're ready too."

"Yeah and I won't be picking up."

"That's alright. You got text, email, and don't think I won't jump in those YouTube comments and tell all of our business."

"You wouldn't!"

"I would. We could be famous. Cosplay Bae and Chef Bae," he said and I closed my eyes laughing, but even as corny as that sounded it was kind of cute too.

"All I'm asking is for you to let me try, Nicole. You're a bad girl, right? You don't love these niggas, right? So what difference would it make? If I fuck up then I prove you right. Or if I don't fuck up then I'm the cherry on top to your already complete life. Either way you win," he reasoned and I actually liked the sound of that. He was the one way to play the game and win either way.

"Well if you would have just explained it that way from the beginning we wouldn't have had to go through all of this, would we?" I laughed out while kissing his lips.

"But I'm not Cam. I love New York too much so I'm not moving for you."

"I'm not Tillar. I'd never let you."

"Are you ready to go in yet?" he asked, but I shook my head no and just asked for one more minute.

"Want me to take your mind off of it?" he asked and I nodded again. "Okay if we were gonna do it, you know get married and have all the bells and whistles for real, how would you want it done?"

"Um...I don't know. I guess I would do it in that big greenhouse you're always posting on Instagram because it looks so pretty at night. We could get some nice lights and maybe even have a meal made out of what was grown in there," I said before noticing him looking down at me. "What?"

"You didn't just freestyle that. You've thought about that before, haven't you?" he asked looking like he was in awe, but instead of answering I just kissed his lips.

"I'm ready to go in now."

He grabbed hold of my hand and led the way in and as soon as we rounded a corner to the waiting room we ran into BJ and a man who looked just like him so I knew it was my father, Bernard Young.

BJ still hadn't noticed me yet, but Bernard's eyes widened and I knew that he knew who I was because he almost spilled the coffee in his hand.

"Is that you Nicki?" he asked, but all I could focus on was how small they both were. Neither could've been more than five-eight so I instantly knew where I got my height from.

"Oh and look at that thick pretty hair. You got that from your mother. You should have seen it before the cancer treatments got to it."

"Is s-she gonna be okay then?" I asked Bernard, but BJ answered.

"Yeah I told her the devil keeps trying to

take her out, but God keeps having the last say."

"You came all this way by yourself?" Bernard asked looking at Chase who was standing behind me now.

"No, a friend brought me," I said pointing over my shoulder.

"I thought I was your fiancé now," he said and I almost winced at that word even though it did accurately describe our situation now.

"Nicki, you're engaged?"

"Yeah it was a spur of the moment thing on the way here. We thought we were dying so he asked," I said downplaying how intense the whole night had been.

"I would've asked her anyway, sir," Chase said as he kissed my forehead.

"You don't do those funny costumes with Nicki, do you?" Bernard asked Chase and it made me smile to know that they had been keeping tabs on me up here. As hard as it had been for me searching for them all this time, it must've also been hard for them to know exactly where I was but still not feel like they could reach out.

"No sir. I'm a chef and owner of a restaurant in Brooklyn."

"Brooklyn is for white people now. That means he's got long money," BJ said chiming in and making everybody laugh before Bernard suddenly began to break down.

He could barely get his words out, but I did hear him ask Chase to take good care of me and it was such a weird patriarchal thing to do, but I let it slide for now.

While we waited for Angela to be able to have visitors, he broke down the story of how I was born then sent to live with Winnie and Henry because they were only fourteen at the time of my birth.

He said that when they got older they considered asking for me back, but that they didn't want to be selfish especially after realizing that they had given their other kids a life that they couldn't give to me. And looking at it from that perspective made it all make sense. If they had kept me then everybody's life would have been so much different. It was tough, but it was definitely the right decision and ultimately I was grateful for it.

"I know Winnie was real strict about celebrating birthdays, but every year she sent us pictures of you like when you made the cheerleading team and when you went off to college," Bernard told me pulling out an old wallet sized picture of me from high school. He also showed me a picture of Angela when she was younger and I definitely saw the resemblance especially at the big floppy afro falling down her back.

"But why didn't you at least reach out when they passed?"

"Angie didn't think it would be fair to you. We had only seen you once since the day we gave you to Winnie and Henry and we didn't want to make it seem like we were trying to replace them."

"Well yeah I get that, but I had a lot of questions around that time and it would have been nice to know."

Before the conversation went any further, a doctor let us know that Angela was ready to be seen but that only one person could go at a time. Bernard offered the spot to me, but I declined because I wanted her to be able to see a friendly face first to prepare her for seeing me.

"Don't be mad at me, but I told her you were on the way yesterday," BJ began. "It was only because she looked like she wanted to give up, but it's like she started fighting again when she knew. So thanks for bringing my mama back to me. Our mama," he said as he got teary eyed. "And this better not be your last trip up here. I gotta show you that I'm the man up here," he bragged like Rochester was the place to be, but I was so overcome with feelings that I didn't even have the words to playfully burst his bubble.

"Only during the summer. Y'all can come visit me in the winter because I'm never doing this again," I said looking at Chase and we both laughed.

Angela was still pretty sedated when I did get to see her, but I wrote her a note and made BJ promise to give it to her when she woke up because I knew I couldn't stay much longer. I was for sure going to miss Tillar's baby shower, but I knew Chase still had stuff to get back to as well.

"Are you ready to leave now? You could still make your meeting if we go."

"We can stay as long as you need," he said thoughtfully. "Just let me see your phone to call Chris and Gram to make sure they're not worried about me because I'm sure they've called by now."

I watched him as he dialed the number and couldn't help but look at how good he looked under the bright hospital lights then wondered if he was actually worth taking a chance on. If I did decide to it wouldn't be as difficult as it seemed because I would probably be visiting my family often and he had already told me that the meeting today was about deciding where he would be running his next restaurant and Atlanta was on the list.

The stars were aligning in our favor and we could reach out and grab them if we wanted. And it was about time I admitted that I wanted to grab them.

"Wait say that again," I heard Chase say in a worried voice as he put my phone on speaker mode.

"It's Gram, Chase. She's gone. They don't know the exact cause yet, but she was unresponsive in bed when they brought in her morning medication. The doctor told me it seemed to be peaceful," I heard Chris's voice say and I could tell this wasn't some cruel joke because it sounded like he had been crying.

I didn't know what to do so I just tried to rub Chase's back in support as he got more details, but unlike that morning he now stepped away from my touch. I tried not to read into it and just let him finish his conversation before I tried comforting him again. He ended the call then handed back the phone without looking directly at me.

"Chase, I am so sorry. I don't even know what to say right now," I said sympathetically, but his voice had that cold distance in it again that I'd first heard from him yesterday.

"Yeah. Look I gotta go. You staying here or coming with me?"

"I'm going with you. And give me the keys. You shouldn't be driving after hearing that," I said going for them, but he snatched away from me.

"I shouldn't have even been here in the first place!"

"Wait what are you saying?"

"I'm saying if I wasn't trying to help you get

here, then I would have been there with her and she would still be here," he snapped at me.

"That's such a fucked up thing to say," I told him on the verge of tears again, but I refused to let them fall this time.

"Yeah well before I take it back let me add to it. How fucked up is it that the mother who didn't even care enough to raise you has a second chance, but my Gram didn't get one?" he asked and I was floored that he was blaming me. I was so mad that I couldn't even think of anything mean to say back.

"Are you just saying this because you're hurting right now or do you really mean that?" I asked, but he didn't answer as he nodded towards the door.

"Are you coming or not?"

"Not," I said simply before taking off the gloves and hat he had given me last night and putting them in his hands. "Drive safe, Chase."

And with that he was gone.

Obviously I hadn't planned on staying, but it was looking like I would for a while so I got BJ's charger so that I could finally call Tillar. I didn't know if Chase or Chris had told them the news yet so I didn't lead with it when she answered.

"Hey I'm so sorry I'm not there, but I promise I'll make it up to you. How's everything going down there?"

"Well from what I saw it was absolutely perfect, but my water broke the second the DJ started playing music so you'll have to ask my guests."

"You're kidding, right?"

"I wish. And those fools are really out there still Cha Cha Sliding while I'm inside having contractions. Good thing the doula was already here or I would be really freaking out right now."

"Have y'all talked to Chase or Chris?"

"No. Wait aren't you with Chase? Oh my God! What happened with your mama and daddy?!"

"Uh…not anymore. He just left. And I need you to focus on getting the baby here safely and I'll be home before you know it, okay?"

"Okay, but first just tell me if they were nice to you."

"Yeah they all were and I'm still waiting for somebody to bring my little sisters up here. It's a gang of niggas here waiting to love on me," I said trying to sound cheerful even though I didn't feel it anymore.

"That's so good. And remember to tell them that they have to take me in too because we're a package deal."

"I will. See you soon. Love you."

After spending a few more hours at the hospital, BJ and my little sisters Renee and Erin decided to have a sibling's road trip to get me back to New York City to catch the flight that I'd booked home. It was fun laughing about stuff and finding out about their lives, but it was bittersweet under the circumstances. The roads weren't all the way clear, but it was still much easier than it was coming.

Before they dropped me off at the airport, I thought about stopping to check on Chase to see if he had calmed down yet, but I decided against it because that's what women like Parker were for.

I found myself asleep on the flight home too and even though I wasn't cold anymore I still wrapped myself up in his coat because it smelled like him and I just wanted to remember how perfect the morning had been.

It was nighttime and there was a baby crying when I walked inside Tillar's house so I wondered if I had lucked up and heard Baby C's first cries, but I knew I hadn't when I saw that she was in bed and had already long given birth. She still looked exhausted though.

But seeing that her, Cam and the baby were all good made me forget all that I'd been feeling before I walked through their door and I walked over with my hands out for him.

"Go wash your hands first," Cam instructed giddily then redirected me to the bathroom.

He was not playing either because there were all kinds of disinfectants in there and hospital scrubs to put on like she hadn't just had a homebirth. I wondered if he knew about his grandmother because he was still on cloud nine from the baby, but I got my answer when I heard them trying to video call somebody.

"She's probably out with her little Deacon boyfriend because Gram never misses my FaceTimes."

I looked at myself in the mirror and felt like crying again, but I just took a deep breath then dried my hands. I couldn't be the one to ruin the happiest day of their life so I would just let them find out from somebody else.

"So how bad did it hurt?" I asked Tillar who looked like she could use a thousand years of rest.

"Enough that Cam felt so bad he agreed to let me name him whatever I wanted," she mused to herself before carefully handing me Cameron Logan III.

"This is literally the longest newborn I've ever seen. He's almost taller than me!" I exclaimed looking at his already pudgy brown face.

"That's not saying much," Cam teased me before answering his ringing phone. It had been going off nonstop since I got there from people still calling to congratulate them on the baby.

Across the room I heard a deep man's voice on the line, but I couldn't tell if it was Chris or Chase. Whichever it was asked a few questions making sure that Tillar and the baby were okay before they must have relayed the news because I saw the silly grin that had been on his face slowly melt away.

"What's wrong? Who was that?" Tillar asked but got no response, but I knew for sure that it was Chase when after suddenly looking over at Tillar and the baby Cam looked at me. And as hard as I tried I couldn't hide the fact that I'd already known.

"I'm sorry," I said then felt Tillar's eyes fall on me because she didn't know what I could possibly be apologizing to him for.

"It's not your fault. It was just her time," he said sadly before saying that he needed a minute to himself.

I explained everything as gently as I could to Tillar, but she still cried and not just because she was fresh off of birth hormones. She loved Miss Ida too and loved that she had welcomed her into the family how she did.

I cried a little too, but I couldn't pretend that my tears were only for that sweet old lady that had always been nice to me because some of them were for her grandson too.

And this was why I never let men in. I

hadn't let one catch me slipping in almost a decade, but this shit here was so unexpected and it hurt like hell. Right then and there I made a promise to myself that no matter what I would never let it happen again.

4

TRAPPILY EVER AFTER

CHASE

When it was all said and done I had decided not to tell Parker about Gram for now. I knew if I did that it would just give her a reason to come back to me and for the first time probably in my adult life I just wanted to be by myself. It was an easy secret to keep too because she was all the way in Westchester with her sister and we'd decided not to have a funeral since Gram had always said she didn't want one.

The idea of people looking in her casket and feeling sad when they saw her made her uneasy and wasn't how she wanted to be remembered. Whenever she would talk about her death, one of us, me, Cam or Chris, would always tell her that she was gonna live forever. But I guess I was the only one who was dumb enough to believe that it was true since she had made it so far.

She was always one of the healthiest people

I knew regardless of age so the fact that a regular ass winter flu had came around and taken her life just didn't sit right with me. But if I was being honest there was no cause of death that would've sat right with me because it was Gram, the only mother I'd ever had.

I felt even guiltier when I realized that not only wouldn't we ever get to celebrate her making it to one hundred, but that I had ruined her ninetieth birthday party by getting into arguments with everybody last Thanksgiving. The only thing that gave me some relief from that painful aching that I'd been feeling since hearing about her death was imagining her up in heaven still trying to cheat in Spades because that was one woman who hadn't ever played by anybody's rules but her own.

The home had a memorial for her so Chris and I went and brought her ashes so that her friends could say their final goodbyes. Cam couldn't make it, but this time I didn't hold it against him because I knew he wasn't taking the whole thing too well and he was still trying to hold it together for Tillar and the baby.

And after putting things in perspective for a couple weeks, I felt really bad about how I had left things with Nicole. I regretted leaving her in Rochester on her own, but more than anything I regretted that I had left at all. I knew she had made it back home safely because I had seen her share a picture of her with Tillar and the baby, but I felt like I had fallen short of what she'd needed on the trip.

She had been waiting her whole life for that moment with her birth parents and it had went better than anybody could have hoped for before I messed it all up. I wanted to apologize, but I didn't even know where to start because it would take more than a simple "My bad" to right a wrong this big.

I had been lying in bed, but for some reason I'd been keeping up with my phone more these days so when it rang on my chest I answered it before it could get to a second ring. I already knew who it was because every day around this time I had been talking to Chris. I guess it was like we knew we had lost the last thing holding us together so we actually needed to start putting in the work to maintain what was left of the Logan Clan. We had decided to finally honor Gram's wishes and put our differences to the side because it was all she had ever really wanted from us.

Her passing had even put a lot of old shit in perspective and I decided not to hold a grudge about all the petty stuff like Cam getting my dad's records anymore. I was trying to start off with a clean slate with my brothers because we had all done wrong to each other over the years including me whether I liked to admit it or not.

"So it's definitely gonna be Atlanta then?" Chris asked about the meeting I'd had with my investor after talking to him yesterday.

"Yeah I go down there this weekend to look at the spot he's got his eye on, but the pictures are cool so I'm already with it."

"So you really think you're LeBron and you're taking your talents down to Atlanta, huh?" he asked and I cracked a smile at what I knew he was hinting at.

"It's just for a little while. After we open my talents will be right back home in Brooklyn."

"You really like her, don't you?" he asked cutting through the minutiae and getting to the point about why I'd suddenly went so hard about making Atlanta the next home of Blaze.

A part of it was honestly because I wanted to be able to spend time getting shit right with Cam while I was there, but I couldn't lie and pretend like the biggest part wasn't because of the little woman that had given me another experience to remember.

"I don't know."

"Nigga yes you do. Just admit that you're about to move down south to open your restaurant and be boo'd up with her and your favorite brother."

"I don't have a favorite brother. Fuck both

of you *Married...With Children* head ass niggas," I joked and Chris laughed so loudly that it got Amber's attention.

"Who's that?" she asked and I could tell that she had come closer because she sounded right next to him now.

"It's Chase whining about your lord and savior Nicole. Remember he said he wants to marry her."

"It wouldn't have been a real marriage," I said reminding him of the part he always left out when he was teasing me about this.

"Ugh stay away from her!" Amber said to me and I couldn't help but laugh because I knew how much she hated the idea of me and Nicole.

And just when I was about to tell her that she didn't have anything to worry about because Nicole wasn't even talking to me, my line beeped from another call coming in. Before my eyes had even finished reading her name on my caller ID, I was barely saying goodbye to Chris and answering after clearing my throat.

"Nicole. Hey. How are you? I mean how have you been?" I asked and felt like a fucking dork for not knowing how to talk to her anymore. But I guess I was breaking new ground here since I had dropped the mean façade and admitted my feelings for her.

"I'm alright, but that's not what I called for.

It's about Cam."

"What about him?" I asked because I had actually spoken to him for a few minutes when I got up that morning. We hadn't been speaking for the same amount of time that Chris and I did, but we were taking baby steps until it felt natural again.

"Well it's just that he's crying a lot and Tillar is worried about him. And I mean I'm here for her, but he doesn't really have anybody here for him since Reese left and I think it would mean a lot if maybe you were here for him," she said then paused for a second, "Chase, your brother really needs you."

"What about you? Do you still need me too?" I asked surprising even myself and apparently her too because she went silent again. "Do you, Nicole?"

"This call isn't about that," she said after sighing. "Are you coming to help him or not?"

"Yeah. He already knows I'm coming Friday anyway because of the restaurant."

"You're really doing it here?" she asked in a neutral voice so I couldn't really determine how she felt about it.

"Yeah it's not official yet, but Atlanta will more than likely be the second home to Blaze," I told her then sat up as I spoke the words that came from my heart next. "And when I get there

Friday and take care of everything with Cam, I hope that we can have a conversation about moving past what happened between us that last day because I'm really sorry about everything."

"I won't be here Friday," she said instead of acknowledging my apology. "I'm going to Japan for Comic-Con."

"How long will you be there?"

"I don't know yet. I'm thinking of turning it into a little vacation because I just need to get away and do something for myself."

"But won't Tillar need you?" I asked even though I really had just wanted her to stay and be in Atlanta when I would be there to make things easier.

"She's the one pushing me to go and her Auntie Diane is coming back to help with everything soon anyway."

"Oh well then I'm happy for you, you know doing this on your own. And maybe when you get back we can have that talk then?" I asked trying to slip it in by any means necessary that we were gonna hash shit out eventually, but her heavy sigh told me all I needed to know.

"I don't think so. We are very different people and it's just like you said. Trying to force two things that aren't meant to be together is just a waste of time."

"But what if they actually are meant to be

together and they're both just too stubborn to make it happen? And I mean I'm a chef so I put opposing shit together all the time. Like for instance, I emulsified the hell out of that oil and eggs for my house mayo that you liked on your sandwich, didn't I?" I asked trying to make her smile, but I didn't hear any evidence of one in her tone.

"I think it's probably best if you just stay Cam's brother to me and I'll just be Tillar's friend to you," she said so definitively that I was at a loss for words because I had just known after everything we had gone through together that we would be able to get back on track when everything calmed down.

"If that's what you really want then okay. I'll respect that," I said before she decided that it was time to end the call.

I sighed as I laid back down on the bed, letting the phone hit the floor because now that I'd gotten the call that I was waiting for I didn't need to monitor it so closely anymore. And it was just so funny that for over a year I had waited for the day where she reached out to me, but neither time had turned out how I had expected or wanted it to go.

♛

Cam had known for almost a week that I would be coming to Georgia, but he still looked surprised to see me when he opened the front door to his new house and let me in. He was holding the baby so when I went to hug him he immediately stepped back and told me to go wash my hands and change my shirt first.

I was hardly ever around babies so I had always forgotten about all of those rules for newborns and germs and shit, but as I was in the bathroom washing up my arms, I was reminded that even at sixteen Cam had us all doing the same shit for Cree when she was born. He was still a kid himself then, but I remembered that the day she was born he had decided to become more than just a dad. He decided to become a man too.

And I knew that I would never be a dad, but upon this realization I told myself that I would start being a real man too because still acting like a boy at my age had caused me to almost lose everything and everybody that really mattered.

After freshening up I walked back through the house the same way I had came in, but I didn't see Cam anywhere. From the outside I knew this place was big as shit so I didn't even bother going on a search. I just called him to guide me to his whereabouts which was outside to a garden he was starting in their courtyard. He had a nice little setup out there with the pool and there was even a chill spot with shade where he was sitting now.

"Ay I can't even front. This is a prime piece of real estate y'all got here. How much did it set you back?" I asked because I knew he was never the type to rent like me or Chris and he'd probably already paid it off in full.

"Trust me. You don't even want to know, but it's all for my other baby in there," he nodded referring to Tillar. "When she's sleeping, I usually just come out here to work in the garden so she won't hear Baby Cam if he cries," he said still trying to keep it together for me too, but I could tell from his sad eyes that he had been crying today.

I told him to sit the baby down in the bouncer for a minute so that I could finally hug him. He sighed before eventually getting up and doing what I had said.

I let him take a few good deep breaths while I held onto him then encouraged him to release whatever it was that he had been holding onto. Almost instantly his tears began falling on the fresh white tee that he had given me to put on at the front door.

"Cree's been on my mind even more than usual lately. And I just hope she knows that I'm not forgetting about her because I still think about her every day. She's still my baby too," he cried out in a way that would break even a stranger's heart let alone mine who had seen firsthand just how much light my niece brought to our lives.

"She knows. That's one thing you never have to worry about," I said trying to console him as I held onto him tighter.

"I just don't know how I'm supposed to be here without Gram, Chase. I mean she was my rock and I'm just so hurt that she didn't get to see me be a dad again."

"You really think Gram's nosy ass ain't already checking in on us? She's up there watching right now with Ma, Dad and Cree. I just hope she gives us a little privacy during showers because that's when I really start feeling myself if you know what I mean," I said being goofy just because I knew he needed it now.

"Yo something is really wrong with you," he said laughing through his tears as he finally let me go and wiped his face.

"I know and I also know that we still got a lot of shit to work through to build up that trust again, but I'mma be down here a lot for a while and I just want you to know that I'll try to be your rock if you need me to be."

"You hardly ever answer your phone so you would make a lousy rock," he began stubbornly now that he was regaining his composure, "but if I need one, I'll let you know and you better pick up."

"No *ifs*. You know your soft ass is gonna need it," I said playfully muffing him while trying to hide my own watery eyes. "But I'm not Gram and I don't want to look at your ugly face all the time so no video chats, alright?" I joked, but he agreed claiming that I looked just like him.

"It's just so hard to believe she's really gone. I keep holding onto my phone expecting her to call."

"I've been doing that too and regretting all those Sundays that I should have spent in church with her instead of at the restaurant."

"Nah. That hard work is what got you where you are now and Gram wanted that for you. For all of us," he said before noticing the baby wiggling around in the bouncer. He went to pick him up, but I asked if I could do the honors.

"So y'all are really calling him Baby Cam?" I asked as I finally picked up the little sleeping giant and he nodded. "You know it used to really piss me off every time I heard people calling you and dad Big Cam and Lil' Cam like me and Chris weren't standing right there."

"That's because you've been a hater all your life."

"Nah, but for real he's too big for me to be calling him a baby. I'm calling my lil' man C3 because he's already mad long and I know he's about to be the first Logan to make it to the league," I said carefully stretching out his arms to see his wingspan, but Cam stopped me.

"That's if he wants to. I just want him to be happy," he said proudly looking down at his seed. "Chris told me you haven't been back to work yet. Still don't feel ready?" he asked me after we had sat back down.

"Nah. You can't really be in the kitchen if your mind is somewhere else," I told him honestly because even though I was technically in town to expand the Blaze brand, food was the last thing I was thinking of.

"Is that why you came down here then, because it's where your mind is?"

"What are you saying?" I smiled already knowing where he was going because if he had talked to Chris about me then he was for sure up to date on the status or lack of status between me and Nicole.

"Are you just doing the restaurant thing or trying to see somebody?" he asked before confessing that he had eavesdropped on Nicole telling her side of things to Tillar.

"Just the restaurant. I tried to talk to her the other day, but she's not interested and I don't really blame her. I fucked up pretty bad and you only get one shot with a woman like that," I said even though it hurt to admit.

"Don't be fooled by that wall she puts up.

Nic is a sheep in wolf's clothing. She just does all that tough shit to protect herself, but inside she's hoping that the right man eventually shows up and proves her wrong."

"Well you know her better than I do. You think I'm the right man for her?"

"Who better than an honorable Logan man?" he asked sarcastically as I adjusted C3 in my arms.

"I'm not really feeling too honorable these days."

"Nah. You and Chris try to run from it, but I think there's more of Dad in y'all than there is in me. Chris gave Amber a whole new life and you tracked down Nic's parents and you're not even taking credit for it. You just did it because you wanted to see her happy. That sounds pretty honorable to me," he said even though I had no idea how he'd found out because that was just one more secret that I had planned on taking to the grave with me.

The same night that Parker had told me she was leaving, I'd planned on doing everything to make her stay including finally kicking my addiction to Nicole. I wanted to go cold turkey. No more video games. No more checking her pages all day. No more her period. But one last visit to her YouTube channel had me coming across a recent video that I had somehow missed and it was a personal one.

She talked for a while about wanting to know her birth parents and where she came from before laying out everything she did know about them. She thanked a few private investigators that had honestly done what they could and found her helpful leads before saying that she had become discouraged lately because she had spent a lot of money on others who led her on for months at a time even though they knew they had reached dead ends.

I knew that I was supposed to be letting her go, but I couldn't help but think about a regular customer of mine that came into Blaze at least a couple times per week. He had been in the newspaper recently for finding a kidnapped kid in a nasty custody battle where even the police couldn't locate their whereabouts. I was positive that all the recent press had made his prices skyrocket, but whatever the cost was I'd wanted to get him on her case to see if I could help out.

And it just so happened that he was the right man for the job because within seven days he had found the information Nicole had been searching for her whole life. Never did I think that she would go see them the second she heard the news, but once she had found herself in New York and determined to get there I knew I had to help by at least giving her the car. But thanks to Gram I had been able to play knight for a night and personally escort her there.

"How did you know it was me?"

"Well I didn't until you just confirmed it, but I knew it was most likely you when I looked up the number that called the store for Nic. It was from a detective agency in Brooklyn just a few blocks away from Blaze," he informed me before making direct eye contact in a way that reminded me of my dad. "You did a good thing, Little Brother and I can't even tell you how proud I am with words," he said sincerely and I felt my body getting warm with emotion.

"The world must be coming to an end. Since when do you sing my praises?" I asked before he sighed.

"Because the last time we argued you made a good point. I'm never giving up the shop life, but you weren't wrong about me idolizing Dad too much so after I came back home I decided to officially step out on my own."

"And how did you do that?"

"I'm surprised Gram didn't tell you, but I'm actually writing a book."

"Like a self-help book? What's it about?"

"Nah. Fiction. And it started off being just about me and Tillar, but then Chris and Amber gave me some inspiration too. And now I'm wondering if you want to give me something good for the last few chapters because it's almost time for Nic to go to the airport. Everybody loves a good airport ending, Chase," he joked, but I shook my head no because I didn't want to be let down again.

"Man stop fronting for me and go get your girl. If you leave now you should just catch her," he told me as I looked down at my watch to see the time before he went on. "You know the night of the ball Gram told Tillar that she would leave here happy if she knew we all had somebody and that got me to thinking. Maybe she decided that she could finally let go when she saw you with Nicole that night because she knew you had somebody. You don't want to disappoint Gram, do you?" he asked laying it on as thick as cold peanut butter.

"Oh c'mon don't do that," I said playfully and pretended to be in pain.

"Whatever. Just give me back my kid because I see you over there calculating how long it'll take you to get to the airport," he said before standing up again and taking C3. "I love you, bro. Now go get her," he nodded towards the door and before I knew it I was out of there and on my way.

It was midday so the traffic in Atlanta wasn't at its worst, but it wasn't at its best either and I prayed for a miracle the whole Uber ride there because I knew if I could just get in front of her one last time, she would see how devoted I was to her.

Gram must've been smiling down on me from heaven and putting in a good word for me with God because the second I got out of the car, I saw Nicole struggling over by the automatic doors.

There was a nearly empty Bean ice coffee cup in her hand holding things up, but she wasn't letting it go until the very last drop. I was so happy to be able to run over to her instead of having to search for her inside because a big black man wildly running through the airport would have gotten me tackled and tased instead of being able to profess my feelings like I wanted to do.

"You need some help with that?" I tried to ask as smoothly as possible, but I was out of breath from the excitement and the short jog over. At the sound of my voice she dropped the cup and the little that was left inside spilled on her suitcase.

"Fuck. Chase, what are you doing here?" she asked me obviously annoyed that the bottom of her expensive luggage was now stained.

"I'm here because I'm a man of my word. I'm still gonna marry you and then divorce you and then try to be a good enough boyfriend to maybe even convince you to eventually marry me for real one day," I told her honestly even though she still refused to look up at me.

But I saw from her eyes that even though I was saying the right things, it still wasn't enough to make her change her mind.

"Look I have a flight to catch. I don't have time for this," she said then successfully grabbed hold of all of her bags since both hands were free now.

"I know you don't so that's why I'm gonna make this quick and easy for you," I told her as I stood in front of her blocking her way inside.

Other people were giving us dirty looks for having to go around us, but I didn't care. This was buzzer beater time and I had to make sure my shot went in because there would be no chance of overtime here.

After a few long seconds she finally looked up at me then let me know that she would listen to what I had to say. I was so happy that I barely got the words out.

"Okay before you go I just want to lay out some ground rules for you because I don't want you over there in Japan playing with anybody else's sushi roll. Whether you like it or not, you're in a relationship now and we're both gonna respect that," I told her as I took her hand in mine.

"A relationship?" she asked incredulously.

"Yep. A real live relationship with yours truly."

"Just like that?"

"Just like that," I repeated.

"And I have no say in this, huh?"

"Nah. Two chefs in the kitchen always messes shit up so I thought that I would go ahead and make this decision for you," I said playfully and I felt so relieved when I saw a small smile peek through.

"And just how would this 'relationship' work with you being all the way in Brooklyn and me being here?"

"Well as you know I just signed off on the new restaurant this morning which means that I'll be here a lot and I know you'll be coming to New York to see your family. Basically someway, somehow we're gonna make this shit work, but we can go over the fine print when you get back," I told her then waited to see her response. She was quiet for a little while like she was honestly considering the whole thing.

"How about this? I'll give you a free trial starting now and you can tell me about these details on the flight to Tokyo. It's about fourteen hours away so I know we'll cover everything by the time we land," she suggested, but before I agreed and got too excited I had to know one thing first.

"Are you asking me to come because you're still scared to go alone?"

"No. I'm asking because I want you to come, but I could definitely use some muscle in case this trip turns into *Hostel: Tokyo Drift*," she joked and I couldn't help but laugh at her.

"Well as much as I would love to go with you right this second, I don't have anything with me so I'll have to catch another flight."

"You have a passport, your wallet and your phone. What else do you need?" she asked then told me nevermind when I began actually listing things.

"No no no. You're right. I don't need anything else. I just need you, Nicole," I told her as I looked into her eyes and finally planted the kiss that I'd been planning since I left Cam's house.

"Well let's see how we do on the flight first because being trapped in a car with you didn't really go over so well," she said then told me to hurry so we could see if there were still any seats on her flight.

Apparently there was only one flight from Atlanta to Japan once per week so the plane was nearly full except for first class so I gladly bought myself a ticket then upgraded hers from business class.

Unfortunately she couldn't get the seat next to me, but I knew my neck would hurt from looking back at her so much because I was still in shock that this was really happening. And she was really about to be my wife, then my ex-wife, then maybe even my wife again someday if I could convince her. But that was a long ways away and for now we would just focus on taking this fairytale one day at a time.

My brothers were lucky enough to have their stories come together in a more traditional way, but I had a feeling that my time with my Rapunzel wouldn't be as easy as it was to let down her hair. I would stick it out for as long as she allowed me to though because sometimes the best happily ever afters were the ones that couldn't be wrapped up neatly in a bow.

Sometimes there wasn't a proposal, a wedding, or a baby. Sometimes it was just two people with a spark trying not to let it set them ablaze. And to me that was better than a perfect ending. That was real life and more than happily ever after, I just wanted a happy *beginning* and a real chance with Nicole to prove that I could be the type of man she thought none of us could be.

I looked back at her one last time before takeoff and she stuck out her tongue at me as she put on her headphones. Instead of returning the gesture I just sighed because I knew all that shit I'd just said was about to go right out the window I was now looking out of. And once she foolishly signed that dotted line agreeing to be Mrs. Logan, she would never be able to get me out of her hair

again because there was nowhere else I'd rather
be.

FOLLOW ME

Thanks for reading! If you don't want to miss out on any updates about future works of mine then find me on all social media platforms as TanSaidWhat.

Visit www.tanzaniaglover.com

And if the cover art took your breath away as much as it did mine, check out the talented artist Bree Douthitt! Thank you so much for bringing Trapunzel to life!

THANK YOUS

I said that I was done writing dissertations to my family and friends in this section so I'll try to keep this brief especially since my love for them has remained the same since the first time I did this. But I do want to say that I feel like the luckiest person in the world to be able to go on this journey with people who genuinely love and care for me. Because of the immense amount of love and support that I receive from them, I get to do the thing I love most in the world and I'm forever grateful for it.

www.ingramcontent.com/pod-product-compliance
Lightning Source LLC
Chambersburg PA
CBHW031540310726
48971CB00008B/2555